Praise for Maria Grace

"Grace has quickly become one of my favorite authors of Austen-inspired fiction. Her love of Austen's characters and the Regency era shine through in all of her novels." ***Diary of an Eccentric***

"Maria Grace is stunning and emotional, and readers will be blown away by the uniqueness of her plot and characterization" ***Savvy Wit and Verse***

"Maria Grace has once again brought to her readers a delightful, entertaining and sweetly romantic story while using Austen's characters as a launching point for the tale." ***Calico Critic***

"I believe that this is what Maria Grace does best, blend old and new together to create a story that has the framework of Austen and her characters, but contains enough new and exciting content to keep me turning the pages. ... Grace's style is not to be missed." ***From the desk of Kimberly Denny-Ryder***

Darcy & Elizabeth Christmas 1811

A Peek Behind the Scenes

Maria Grace

White Soup Press

Published by: White Soup Press

Darcy & Elizabeth: Christmas 1811
Copyright © December 1, 2017 Maria Grace

For information, address
author.MariaGrace@gmail.com

ISBN-13: **978-0-9980937-5-8** (White Soup Press)

Author's Website: RandomBitsofFaascination.com
Email address: Author.MariaGrace@gmail.com

Dedication

For my husband and sons.
You have always believed in me.

✣Intoduction

JANE AUSTEN TELLS us almost nothing of what transpired during the Christmas Darcy and Elizabeth spent prior to their marriage near the end of 1812. What might have happened those months that Darcy spent in London whilst the militia wintered in Meryton?

Take a peek behind the scenes Austen wrote into what might have been

✤ Chapter 1

November 24, 1811 Stir it up Sunday. Meryton

SUNDAY MORNINGS BEFORE holy services were usually a calm restful time in the Bennet household. The early-rising members of the family would gather in the parlor to read or sew, whilst the late ones—usually Lydia and Kitty—would dash in just before it was time to go, laughing and merry and gay.

This, the last Sunday before advent, was different somehow. Was it just the presence of their uninvited and, at least in Elizabeth's mind, unwelcome guest that changed everything? It was hard to say, but she was tempted to believe it.

Papa proved hard to ignore as he paced along his favorite track in the parlor, back and forth in front of the fireplace whilst the rest of the family assembled.

Elizabeth pressed her lips hard and turned her face aside. He would know she was trying not to laugh at his impatience if he caught sight of her.

Jane sat near the window with her needlework. A low fire warmed the room almost as much as the sunbeams through the window that danced along the carpet and cast shadows on the yellow wall near the chair where Elizabeth sat. The sun had faded the upholstery to be sure, but it was also very warm and friendly, a necessary quality in a room where the family gathered.

Papa passed by her again, the scent of his shaving soap reached out and tickled her nose—a funny, sneezy herbal scent. "Mrs. Bennet, we await your presence." He stared at the doorway as though that might bring her in faster.

"You know she always takes particular care with her Christmas pudding preparations." Elizabeth went to him.

He huffed and wrinkled his lips into a special frown reserved for Mama alone. "How long does it take to pour some brandy over fruit and spices?"

She patted his arm and followed him as he tramped back along his path. "You know as well as I, it is more complex than that."

Jane joined them near the fireplace. "Stoning and chopping the fruit is time consuming."

"Is that not why we employ Hill and Cook? As I recall, she took great pride in telling Mr. Collins that you girls did not sully yourselves with toiling in the kitchen."

Why did Papa have to mention *him*? Elizabeth cringed. "Indeed she did, but Christmas pudding is no regular food stuff."

"You know how special Christmas pudding is to her," Jane said.

"Would that it be special on a day of the week with nowhere else demanding our presence." He shook his head and rolled his eyes toward the ceiling where the maid had missed a spot in her dusting.

Mr. Collins, Mary in his shadow, trundled in. "Good day to you, Mr. Bennet, and to you, my fair cousins."

Necessary pleasantries were exchanged, and Elizabeth sidled away. With a little good fortune, his attentions might continue toward Mary, and she could escape his notice.

"I was just telling Mr. Collins about Mama's great love of Christmas pudding, and how she loves this Sunday above all others." Mary threw a hopeful look toward Mr. Collins.

Mr. Collins thumbed his lapels, expression sober, almost severe. Why did he always have to take the role of the authority on nearly everything—especially when he seemed to know so little? "As a clergyman, I am not certain—"

"Excuse me. I need to speak to Mrs. Bennet." Papa edged past them and out of the parlor.

Elizabeth peeked into the corridor. He turned toward his study not the kitchen. She squeezed her eyes shut and sighed. Though she could not really blame him, it would have been more polite for him not to abandon them to his relation.

Mr. Collins looked after him, his brows drawn tight together, as though unable to work out why Papa might have left. His shoulders twitched in a tiny shrug, and he turned back to his remaining, captive audience.

"I am not certain how this particular Sunday holds any significance above others. Surely the Sundays of Advent—"

"Mama finds the day has personal significance, not doctrinal importance." Jane's tone was so soft and reasonable. What a shame to waste it on one who was not.

Mr. Collins formed a silent 'o' as if the idea of personal significance were an entirely new concept.

Elizabeth and Jane took to the settee. Elizabeth picked up her sewing from the basket and ducked her head. Perhaps he would not take notice of her.

Lydia and Kitty skipped in, giggling and tittering about the bonnet that Lydia had newly trimmed.

"Why should this Sunday have such personal import that she might be at liberty to make the entire family late to holy services?" Mr. Collins clasped his hands behind his back and resumed Papa's path, pacing before the fireplace.

"Are you going to tell the story of Mama and Papa's betrothal?" Lydia snickered.

"What has that to do with this particular Sunday?"

"The Christmas pudding that foretold their betrothal—" Kitty glanced at Lydia.

"Was stirred up on this day—" Lydia grabbed Kitty's hand.

"And Mama was the one who put the ring charm in the pudding," they finished together.

"She looks fondly upon Christmas puddings as a result." Mary mimicked one of Mama's warning glances toward Kitty and Lydia, but failed to achieve the desired effect.

"Fondly? Only fondly?" Lydia chortled. "She considers them essential and auspicious, slaving over them each year as though—"

"Your mother declares herself ready—let us be off," Papa called from the vestibule.

Lydia and Kitty led the procession out. Mr. Collins lingered behind near the settee.

The back of Elizabeth's neck prickled. Why was he looking at her like that?

Thankfully, the carriage was not required for the trip to church. A fine brisk walk in the morning sun and crisp breeze was exactly what Elizabeth most needed right now. More properly, it would have been what she most needed had Mr. Collins not taken the opportunity to appoint himself as her devoted escort. He immediately took to her side, rescuing her from any danger of reflection or contemplation.

Instead, she became well acquainted with Lady Catherine's beneficence; her prescriptions by which sermon writers might offer the most appropriate sermons for parishioners; her magnanimous assistance in reviewing the sermons he himself wrote; her generous refinements added to his preparations.

Heavens, could the man not think nor act for himself?

"Is it truly necessary to have her review your work, sir? Forgive me if I am incorrect in my understanding, but is not a vicar secure in his position? Why is her favor so significant?" She scuffed her toes in the dirt as she walked.

Such a glance he cast upon her! So condescending! No one had looked at her that way since she was an overly inquisitive little girl.

"It does you credit, dear cousin, that you would give so much consideration to my situation. You are quite correct in your understanding of the nature of my preferment. Nothing short of complete moral failure on my part can separate me from it. I flatter myself to believe it entirely avoidable on my part."

"I am sure you are correct. Still, I do not apprehend your most profound devotion to her opinion." She kicked a dry clod of dirt out of the path.

"Is it not a right and pleasing thing to be concerned for the opinion of those whom Providence has placed in superior positions? One can profit both spiritually and in more temporal ways from their beneficence."

"Oh, now I see." He was a puppy, begging for crumbs at her table. To be fair, his income could not be much above a tenth of Papa's, but still. Had he no dignity?

She shifted her wrap to soothe the prickles across the back of her neck. What he implied was too much like a servant holding out a hand for vails from houseguests. Would he expect the same obsequiousness from a wife? No doubt he would. She swallowed hard.

The church bells rang a final call to worship as they arrived and went directly to their worn wooden pew. The little stone and wood church brimmed with congregants. How utterly unsurprising that Mr. Collins should contrive to sit between her and Jane.

The vicar read the day's prayer. "Stir-up, we beseech thee, O Lord, the wills of thy faithful people; that they, plenteously bringing forth the fruit of good works, may of thee be plenteously rewarded; through Jesus Christ our Lord. Amen."

Lydia elbowed Kitty and whispered, "Stir up, we beseech thee, the pudding in the pot. And when we do get home tonight, we'll eat it up hot."

Elizabeth stifled a laugh.

"I suppose it is the fashion of young people today to freely parody those things considered sacred. I am pleased to see that you do not indulge in such unseemly fancies," Mr. Collins muttered under his breath, eyes fixed on the vicar.

Elizabeth bit her lip hard. Bother. She would have been better served laughing heartily. Perhaps that might have given him pause instead of one more thing to fuel his unseemly praise of her. What beastly luck to have herself in proper check this morning.

Mr. Collins offered his reflections and commentary on the sermon throughout the service. In short, the vicar executed his task admirably enough, but his sermon was too modern. He would have clearly benefited from the guidance a patron like Lady Catherine could offer. It was difficult not to wonder if Mr. Collins would have appreciated such a critique from one of his own congregants.

Her skin itched and every limb twitched. She would have gasped for breath had it not been likely to gain even more attention from him. His presence had all the appeal of a coarse wool blanket on bare skin.

Mama glanced at them from the far end of the pew. Prim and entirely satisfied, she folded her hands in her lap and peeked first at the Bingleys across the aisle, then the Lucases to whom she offered a well-pleased smile.

How shocking to be so self-congratulatory in church! Elizabeth's stomach churned. It had not been a misunderstanding as Jane insisted. Mama clearly expected, even anticipated, Mr. Collins making an offer to one of her girls. Not just one of her girls, but to Elizabeth in particular.

Surely, even Mama could see how unsuitable they were to one another. Surely he could see it, too. No man could be that insensible, could he?

On the way home, Mary contrived to walk with Mr. Collins. How she managed—and why—were a mystery, but Elizabeth enjoyed the fruits nonetheless. She strolled beside Jane, savoring the quiet company and gentle sunshine as their half-boots crunched among the dry leaves. With Mr. Collins behind her, she could nearly block out the sound of his voice in favor of the sounds of the countryside—birds, sheep, cows and a few horses.

Mama faded back from her place beside Papa and interposed herself between Elizabeth and Jane. How did she manage to arrange her generous rust-colored skirts to seem all fluffed and prickly like an angry hen? Even the fur on her muff seemed to be standing on end. "It is not becoming for you to roll your eyes so much, Lizzy. I have seen you do it far too often recently."

"Yes, Mama."

"And another thing. I do not much like your way of constantly escaping Mr. Collins's most agreeable company. See there, Mary is walking with him. It should be you." Mama glanced over her shoulder, none too discreetly.

Jane leaned toward Mama. "I do believe Mary is partial to Mr. Collins's society."

"I do not care what Mary's preferences are. Mr. Collins deserves more than a plain middle child. Since

he cannot have the eldest, his preference falls to you."
She elbowed Elizabeth sharply.

"Mary would much rather have it." Elizabeth
peeked over her shoulder. "And he does not seem
much displeased for it." In all likelihood, any of them
would do for him; he hardly seemed to care very
much which.

"That is because he is a gentleman and does not
wear his heart upon his sleeve. Do not be insensible
of the great boon he seeks to be to all of us."

"Are you telling me—"

"It seems I can tell you nothing, obstinate girl. I
am simply reminding you of the reality of our situation, something you would be wise not to forget."
Mama waved a pointing finger just under Elizabeth's
chin and marched back to her place beside Papa.

Elizabeth hesitated a few steps, increasing the distance between her and Mama. "Oh, Jane. What am I
to do?"

"Do not be too hard on Mama. You know her
nerves."

"Papa's great friend all these years? Yes, I well
know her nerves." She rolled her eyes. Perhaps Mama
did have a fair point on that account.

"Do be fair, or at least try."

"I try. Indeed, I do. But what sense does it make
to deny Mary her preference and me mine? You and I
have always agreed we should marry for love alone."

Jane sighed and glanced in the direction of Netherfield Park. "Yes, it is a very desirable thing. But not
everyone is the same. Mr. Collins's motivations seem
very different. Not wrong, but different."

"So different, I do not see how I may bridge the
gap—nor do I see why I should when things might

very well be agreeably settled with Mary."

"She does seem to take great pains to seek out his company. Perhaps he and Mama may be made to see reason."

Hopefully Jane was correct. But what if she were not?

Even if it were not possible to marry for love, it should not be too much to ask to be able to enjoy a friendship with the man she married, should it? How could she possibly settle for less than that?

After a light nuncheon in the dining room, Mama called them all to the kitchen. She had done the same thing every Stir it Up Sunday since Elizabeth could remember. The large worktable in the center of the kitchen bore the fragrant makings of the pudding. The air swirled with the fragrances of brandy and spices hanging in the steam of the great roiling cauldron waiting to accept the finished pudding.

"You too, Mr. Collins, for you are part of the family, to be sure." Mama waved him toward the table.

He edged in between Jane and Elizabeth.

Of course, where else might he stand?

Elizabeth sidled over to make room for him, nearly treading on Mary's toes in the process. Poor Mary looked so dejected. If only they might switch places, but Mama would no doubt cause such a scene if they did.

"Now, Mr. Collins has it been the habit of your family to make a Christmas pudding?" Mama asked.

"This is the first time I have experienced this most charming and agreeable custom, madam. To be sure, the Christmas puddings at Rosings Park—"

"Well then, I shall tell you how we do it. There is a great bowl there, and you each have the ingredients beside you. You, sir, have the flour. Add it to the bowl and then pass it east to west."

"Clockwise," Papa whispered loudly.

Apparently, he thought little of Mr. Collins's sense of direction. Probably for good reason.

"Yes, yes like that. Give the bowl to Jane now."

She added a pile of minced suet and passed it to Kitty. Kitty and Lydia added dried fruits and nuts and passed it into Papa's hands for the bread crumbs and milk.

Mama poured in the brandy soaked citron and spices. "And that makes eleven ingredients. We have two more now, thirteen for Christ and the apostles."

Mary added the eggs and slid the heavy vessel to Elizabeth.

"How fitting for you to add the final sweetness, Cousin Elizabeth."

Elizabeth nearly spilled the sugar.

Mama glowered at her, but quickly recovered her composure and handed Mr. Collins the wooden spoon. "To remind us of the Christ child's crib. Now stir it east to—clockwise—with your eyes closed sir. And make a wish."

Mr. Collins steadied the bowl and grasped the spoon. "I shall wish for—"

"No, sir," Elizabeth forced herself not to roll her eyes. Unfortunately, Mama would never notice what she had not done. "Your wish must be made in silence."

Mama glowered again. Little matter though. Elizabeth had no desire to hear Mr. Collins's wish. His expression said too much as it was.

The bowl passed around the table. Some wishes were easy to guess.

Mary wished to be noticed by Mr. Collins. Kitty and Lydia wished to be noticed by anyone but Mr. Collins. Mama doubtless wished Mr. Collins to marry one of her girls, preferably Elizabeth. Jane, of course, wished for Mr. Bingley. But Papa's wish remained a mystery. What would he want?

The cold, heavy bowl passed to her. The rough wooden spoon scraped at her fingers. What to wish for? She closed her eyes and forced the spoon through the heavy batter. *To marry for love. I wish to marry for love.*

"Do not dawdle so, Lizzy. We must add the charms now. Here one for each of you." Mamma passed a charm to each sister and Mr. Collins. "Add your charm to the pudding and stir it again."

Mama shoved the bowl toward Mary. "You start."

Mary gulped. "I have the thimble—"

"How fitting. Spinsterhood!" Lydia snickered.

"It is for thrift." Jane's tone was as firm as it ever got, a veritable rebuke.

"For thrift, then." Mary tossed it in and quickly worked it into the batter.

"I wonder which of us shall travel." Lydia tossed a tiny shoe charm into the pudding.

"And which shall find safe harbor?" Kitty followed with an anchor and held the bowl while Lydia folded them in.

Jane added the coin and Elizabeth the horse shoe. Jane held whilst Elizabeth stirred.

"And you Mr. Collins?" Mama blinked, but her expression was far from innocent.

"It seems I have the ring." He dropped it into the pudding, eyes on Elizabeth.

"How very auspicious. Did you know, I added that same charm to a Christmas pudding the year of my betrothal to Mr. Bennet?"

"Traditions says—and I would hardly count it accurate—that the finder of the ring will wed, not the one who dropped it in the pudding," Papa muttered.

Did Mama rebuke him for rolling his eyes the way she had Elizabeth?

"Well that may be, Mr. Bennet, it might be. But, I can speak to what happened for me. I believe it may well have significance for others among us." Mama fluttered her eyes at Mr. Collins.

Mr. Collins smiled his cloying smile and edged a little closer to Elizabeth.

Papa huffed softly. "Let us hope that something with greater sense than a pudding prevails over such decisions, shall we now? So then, give me the buttered cloth and the pudding that it may be tied up and done with."

Elizabeth stood back to give him room to dump the pudding out and wrap it in the pudding cloth.

Thankfully she had an ally in Papa or at least she seemed to. The way Mama carried on and encouraged Mr. Collins, she would need one.

Chapter 2

November 27, 1811. Meryton

MONDAY PASSED QUICKLY with last minute repairs to Kitty's ball gown requiring a pleasing amount of time and energy spent in the company of her sisters and away from Mr. Collins. Pity such good fortune could not have extended the rest of the week and into the Netherfield Ball. He dogged her every step like a hound—no, more like a gosling trailing after a mother goose. Worse still, he proved an indifferent dancer at best, and his manners! Ugh! Could he have done a more thorough job at humiliating himself—and by extension her —before Mr. Darcy?

Following such a performance the previous evening, she could hardly hope to be left in peace today.

She must find it now, whilst everyone else slept, for there would be none once the family awoke. What other reason to be out and about at such an early hour the morning after a ball?

The morning was cold and wet, and rather disagreeable, all told—just cold enough to leave her nose red and tingly. Clouds hung low in the sky, grey and somber, as though the sun could not be bothered to try to peek through. A few birds called, not the pretty songbirds, but the cawing crows whose cry was more ominous than appealing. The brown and crunchy landscape seemed uniformly dreary, with none of the footpaths near the house calling to her. Even the little wilderness near the house felt dull and lifeless. Traces of wood smoke on the breeze failed to smell friendly and inviting, instead they proved scratchy and irritating. But still, the landscape had the very great advantage of being entirely without Mr. Collins. That was enough to make up for nearly every other fault.

Dew collected along the hem of her skirts as she briskly trod the path up Oakham Mount. She lifted her petticoats slightly to avoid another patch of mud. At least the rain itself had obliged and went its way the day before. A slender branch slapped at her face. She snapped it off and slashed at the tall grasses tangling with her skirts, as tenacious in their attentions as Mr. Collins.

"I cannot believe the obstinacy of the man," she muttered. "He has all the social grace of a leech. If he should ever even think ..."

Think? Was there any doubt as to what his intentions were? Only a blind man might mistake them—or one as bent on ignoring the inconvenient and uncomfortable as Papa.

"Why must Mama push so hard and insist upon what she does not truly understand. I know why she thinks it a good thing—but so soon? How can she think she knows his character? It is certainly not the same thing as knowing his position. How am I ever to convince her only a fool dares rush into an alliance no matter how ideal it seems."

He was to leave soon. If she could just continue avoiding him a while longer. Perhaps, Mama might be worked on in his absence to promote Mary's cause as a most willing substitute. Then when Mr. Collins returned as he had threatened …

She cast the branch aside. Yes, that was the best plan, but how was she to avoid him for now?

Surely the tenants needed to be called upon today—that should keep her out all morning. Then she might pay an afternoon call to Miss Goulding. Mr. Collins had, after all, stepped on her dress. That should take up most of the day. Only two more days to fill.

Oh, yes! There would be dinner at Lucas Lodge as well. Charlotte could be counted on to distract him then. That would do very well for everyone.

She paused and leaned back against a large elm. Even if she were successful in avoiding Mr. Collins's attentions now and turning him towards Mary in the future, how could she persuade Mama to leave off her quest to see Elizabeth married to the first available gentleman?

A fly buzzed past her face. She slapped it away.

Was she expecting too much? Did she owe it to her family to accept an obsequious man whose conversation she could hardly tolerate just because the estate was entailed upon him? Some would certainly argue it was her duty.

Jane was so good and obliging, she might be willing to martyr herself so, but she had hopes of Mr. Bingley.

Mr. Bingley!

Jane had a very good chance of marrying well and saving them all just as certainly as if Elizabeth married Mr. Collins.

She gulped in a deep breath. The weight of their future was not wholly on her shoulders after all.

Best return to the house now lest Mama have too much opportunity to make plans for her. She turned back down the path for Longbourn.

Darcy laced his hands behind his head and stared at the deep red curtains. Rosy rays of dawn crept around the heavy woolen panels and illuminated Netherfield's finest guest room. A cheery fire lit the neat, functional chamber, entirely appropriate to an older country manor. Dark stained paneling covered the walls, a fitting backdrop for the imposing mahogany furnishings. The bed linens were fine and soft; the mattresses piled high, all properly aired, with none of that musty smell that often permeated little-used rooms.

Nothing to Pemberley of course, but no reason it should be, either. He stretched under the blankets, working out an annoying knot in his calf. That must have come from dancing last night.

Perhaps the Netherfield ball had been a good idea after all. Despite protestations that Bingley demanded the impossible of her, Miss Bingley had arranged a first-rate event. Probably the best the sleepy little market town had ever experienced.

A pleasant, country affair where one could dance with a partner and not fear it would find its way into the society pages the next day. What was there not to appreciate about that? Certainly, such an event was a novelty he might be willing to repeat.

What a difference a pair of fine eyes and a clever wit could make in what otherwise might have been a dreadful social obligation.

A sharp gust of wind blew in around an ill-fitting window, fluttering the curtains. Fanciful shadows danced about the chamber. The maid had missed a corner in her dusting. He ought to mention it to the housekeeper himself. Miss Bingley might well have the poor girl sacked for the oversight.

Despite Miss Bingley's constant admonishments to the maids, improvement only came when Elizabeth had stepped in during Miss Bennet's illness. How patient she had been with the scullion assigned to make up the fire in Miss Bennet's room.

He screwed his eyes shut and threw an arm over his eyes. Not again! Why could he not shake the thoughts of her from his mind?

Maddening, utterly maddening.

He rolled to his feet and shrugged on his dressing gown. Perhaps a walk around the grounds would help him clear his mind. Unless of course he should encounter her along the way. While it might not be likely, it was exactly the sort of bad luck that he seemed to attract since meeting the Bennets.

Why did she have to be so engaging when her family was so wholly dreadful?

He rang the bell for his valet.

They were truly the worst examples of every offensive vice. Indolent and disconnected, Mr. Bennet ignored anything that might demand exertion: his estate, his wife, his daughters. He settled for what came and made no effort to shape what was to come. With the power to command so much for good, Bennet still chose his own ease over caring for those under his wings. What a revolting connection.

And to shame his own daughter in public, even one as insipid as Miss Mary Bennet! If anyone deserved his censure, it was his horrid wife. Darcy shuddered and brushed the revulsion off his shoulders.

His valet entered and initiated the mechanics of his morning ablutions.

To be fair, Mrs. Bennet shared much in common with the match-making mamas of the *ton*. Most were every bit as determined as Mrs. Bennet to see their daughters successfully wed. But few could match that woman's vulgarity, speaking loudly of Bingley as though he were already shut up in the parson's pound with Miss Bennet.

The unfettered spleen!

At least the mamas of the *ton* had fortunes sufficient to cover their bad manners, giving them the form of respectability, if not the substance thereof. Mrs. Bennet had not even that thin veil to hide beneath.

Darcy gave his jacket a final tug and dismissed his valet with a nod.

Could Bingley afford such a disagreeable association?

Connection to a landed family, even a very minor one, would be good for him and help establish his position in society. Surely, though, there were other eligible girls who would not bring disagreeable baggage with them.

After last night, it would be difficult to convince Bingley of it. The cakey sot was utterly bewitched by his principal partner of the evening. He would probably be on his way to Longbourn to call upon her yet this morning.

How could he make Bingley understand? Old money and an established place in society, like Darcy's, could weather the improprieties of a family like the Bennets. Bingley's fragile social standing could not.

Perhaps something would come to him over breakfast.

He made his way downstairs. Servants bustled about, still working to restore order after the prior night's festivities. Darcy dodged around their efforts and ducked into the morning room.

The east facing room caught the sun, making for pleasant warmth. It probably was dreadfully hot in full summer, though. The round table was a bit over-sized for the room. Whether that meant it was crowded or cozy was probably directly related to how much one appreciated the company sharing the space.

Pleasing scents of fresh breads and meats wafted from the buffet opposite the windows. Platters and serving bowls lay spread along the sideboard with pots of coffee and tea nearby. Coffee's bitter bite suited the morning time well. Tea was better for afternoon and evening.

"Good morning, Mr. Darcy." Miss Bingley rose and curtsied.

Interesting that she should be up so early the day

after a ball and have breakfast already laid out. Most women in her position would have slept well past noon.

"Good morning." He bowed and seated himself along the opposite side of the table. The sun on his back would likely become uncomfortable quickly. At least it was a good reason to cut the meal, and time spent in her company, short.

"I wonder that you are up so early sir, did you not sleep well?"

"It is the habit of a lifetime. I rarely sleep after sunrise."

Everything in her expression begged to be asked a reciprocal question. But questions like that had the unfortunate tendency to lead to highly improper conversations. So he raised his eyebrow and cocked his head.

She blinked several times, clearly waiting for the desired query.

Darcy strode to the sideboard and poured a cup of coffee.

She added sugar to her tea and stirred it silently.

He could go on for the entirety of breakfast this way, comfortable in the silence. In fact, it would be preferable.

"I hardly slept at all last night. I am sick with worry for Charles." Miss Bingley pressed her hand to her chest and leaned back with a sigh.

Drama belonged in the theater, not in the morning room.

"Has he taken ill?"

"After a fashion. Do you not consider him love-sick over Miss Jane Bennet?" Miss Bingley buttered a slice of toast.

How peculiar she should be considering the same things as he. Peculiar and uncomfortable.

"He paid her uncommon amounts of attention last night." He sipped his coffee. Bitter and a bit stronger than he preferred.

"Indeed he did, and I loath to think what it might mean for all of us. You know how impulsive Charles can be."

"True enough, but he falls out of love nearly as quickly as he falls in. Are you not a bit premature in your concerns?"

Miss Bingley balanced her forehead on her fingers. "He seems utterly besotted with her, more so than I have seen him with any other. To be sure Miss Bennet is a good sort of girl—who could object to her alone? But her family?"

Darcy lifted an open hand. "I observed the same spectacle. Best not recount it."

"I could not agree more. Oh, the vulgarity! Can you imagine—of course there is no need as you saw it all yourself. I need not convince you of the very great misfortune of being connected to such people. Charles, though—he has no notion."

"I quite agree." The words sounded so strange, tumbling from his mouth. Agreeing with Miss Bingley? He would have wagered that such a thing would never happen.

"I knew you would see it the same way. We think so alike, you and I." Why was she batting her eyes?

He clutched the edge of his chair lest he bolt from the room.

"Louisa and Hurst quite agree as well. Though Hurst cannot be roused to think it an urgent matter, Louisa and I are convinced we must act quickly. We must persuade him to leave this place at once."

"But you have only just hosted your ball. There will be many anxious to return the invitation. Dinners, parties—"

"I am well aware and dreading nearly every one of them. The society here is boorish and confined at best. The thought of all those engagements is an untold evil. I would endure them for propriety's sake, of course. But each one presents a grave danger of putting Charles in Jane Bennet's company."

Though perhaps a bit alarmist, her reasoning was sound.

"I see no choice but to separate them, for he will give her up no other way." She sipped her tea.

Darcy drummed his fingers on the table. "Are you certain such drastic means are required? I have never found him so difficult to sway."

"Ordinarily, I might agree. I have seen you work your persuasion upon him to great effect. But in this, the risk is too great, and the possibility of him being stubborn, too real. I fear drastic measures must be taken. It is bad enough that there is no way I can prevent him from calling upon Longbourn before he goes to London this morning."

Was it impossible for her to think something out clearly? Did all her thoughts run in convoluted circles? Darcy gripped his forehead. "If he is going immediately to London, I do not see the problem. They will be separated as you desire."

"He will return in just a few days, though, perhaps with strengthened sentiments because he fancied himself lonely whilst he was gone." She leaned forward and tapped the table. "What I propose is this. He will go to London today, and tomorrow we will all join him. Once there, we might begin to work upon him. He regards your insight very highly. If he were to hear you in agreement with us, it would convince him of the evils of returning to the country."

Darcy had never sided with Miss Bingley against her brother before. Usually, he only interfered when Bingley asked his counsel. While it was true, Bingley relied upon him often, it was hard to conscience such open collusion.

"You know how my brother enjoys the diversions of London. Once settled there, you can have no doubt of his happiness." She batted her eyes, again.

He turned aside.

Still, it was for Bingley's own good that it should happen. The sooner, the less painful the ending of the attachment for all involved.

"Very well, I will prepare to leave tomorrow."

Miss Bingley clasped her hands before her chest. "I cannot thank you enough."

Pray, no more batting eyes or fluttering hearts!

Darcy rose and excused himself. If he were to be leaving Netherfield soon, then a morning walk, and on the off chance, an encounter with Miss Elizabeth Bennet, might not be so very dangerous a thing after all. He called for his hat and coat.

Two days of dry weather had done little to reduce the puddles and patches of mud still riddling the footpath. Pemberley's footpaths were much better maintained than these. Little surprise. Netherfield's owner neglected so many details of his estate. Still, the crisp air proved bracing, and no amount of neglect could diminish the morning sunshine. If he closed his eyes, he could almost smell Pemberley.

A flash of color caught his eye—a familiar shade

of blue. Elizabeth had worn that color when she had stayed with her sister at Netherfield

It was her! Walking, no storming up the other side of the path, just beyond a stand of trees. She broke a small branch and slashed at the knee-high grasses reaching for her skirts. Her brows drew together, and she murmured under her breath.

What was she saying? Perhaps if he drew nearer.

He ducked behind a large tree and pressed his back to the trunk.

"I cannot believe … if he should ever …" If only she would enunciate more clearly whilst she talked to herself!

He held his breath and closed his eyes.

"Why must Mama push so hard and insist on what she truly does not understand? I know why she thinks it a good thing, but so soon? How can she think she knows his character? It certainly is not the same thing as knowing his position. How am I to convince her only a fool rushes into an alliance, no matter how ideal it seems?"

She cast the branch aside and stalked away.

So, Miss Elizabeth saw it too. The insidious matchmaking attempts by her mother, and she agreed no good would come of them. She wanted to see her sister separated from Bingley.

Perhaps she might never know of it, but he would perform this service for his friend and for her. On the morrow they would be off to London and make sure Bingley never returned to Netherfield.

Mama met her just outside the small wilderness near the house. "Where have you been? I have been

looking for you for nearly an hour."

More likely it was a quarter hour. Mama's sense of time was notoriously linked to her level of vexation.

"Hill knew I had gone walking."

"Walking? Walking? Who goes walking the morning after a ball?"

"I walk every morning, why should this one be different?"

"Because you are wanted in the house immediately."

"Wanted? What for?"

"Never you mind that. Just come along." Mama grabbed her wrist and dragged her back to the house.

She nearly stumbled and fell. A suffocating pressure gripped her chest.

"I ... I must call upon the tenants." She pulled her hand back, but Mama did not release her.

"You have far more important business to attend. The tenants can wait." Mama flung open the front door and marched in, Elizabeth still trailing behind her. "Now come to the morning room for breakfast."

"When has breakfast become such an urgent endeavor?"

"No more of your cheek girl, go in and sit. Eat with your sister."

Elizabeth sat beside Kitty and pretended interest in a slice of slightly burnt toast.

Mr. Collins entered the room with great solemnity. "May I hope, Madam, for your approbation when I solicit for the honor of a private audience with your fair daughter, Elizabeth, in the course of this morning?"

Elizabeth jumped to her feet.

So did Mama, clapping her hands in front of her

chest. "Oh, dear! Yes, certainly. I am sure Lizzy will be very happy. I am sure she can have no objection. Come, Kitty, I want you upstairs."

Elizabeth clutched the back of her chair. "Dear Mama, do not go. I beg you will not go. Mr. Collins must excuse me. He can have nothing to say to me that anybody need not hear. I am going away myself."

Mama rapped her knuckles on the table. "No, no nonsense, Lizzy. I desire you will stay where you are. I insist upon you staying and hearing Mr. Collins."

Elizabeth dare not disobey so direct an injunction. Perhaps getting this over quickly was the best alternative.

Mama and Kitty walked off, leaving Mr. Collins to begin.

Could a man use more words to say less? His horrifying proposal waxed on until she nearly bit through her tongue. When at last she could loose it, her efforts were of little avail. He denied her at every turn. To such perseverance in willful self-deception Elizabeth could make no reply. Immediately and in silence she withdrew—what other choice had she?

Not a quarter of an hour later, a servant fetched her to her father's study and shut the door behind her. Mama stood primly near the fireplace whilst Papa rested pensively in his favorite chair.

"Come here, child." He beckoned her to his side. "I have sent for you on an affair of importance. I understand that Mr. Collins has made you an offer of marriage. Is it true?"

"Yes, Papa."

"Very well, and this offer of marriage you have refused?"

"I have, sir." She bit her lip and clutched her

hands tightly before her.

"Very well. We have now come to the point. Your mother insists upon your accepting. Is it not so, Mrs. Bennet?"

Mama stepped forward and punctuated her words with her hands. "Yes, or I will never see her again."

Papa chewed his cheek and adjusted his glasses. "An unhappy alternative is before you Elizabeth."

She held her breath.

"From this day you must be a stranger to one of your parents. Your mother will never see you again if you do not marry Mr. Collins, and I will never see you again if you do."

She exhaled heavily and mouthed 'thank you' as Mama sputtered and stammered and stamped.

Of course, Papa would support her—she hardly imagined anything else. But their immediate dismissal from his library stung. Could he have not exerted himself just a little more on her behalf, rather than leaving Mama stalking her from room to room, pleading, cajoling and even at length, threatening for her cause. Only Charlotte's visit took Mama from her side.

By the end of the day, Mr. Collins pleaded Mama cease her lamentations and her insistence upon remedying the situation. His favors were officially withdrawn.

A man who could change his mind with so little effort surely could not have been much affected by sentimentality. Any affection he might have had for her must have been a work of his imagination. Surely this justified her decision, proved beyond doubt his unsuitability for her.

Did it not?

Something in the disappointment in Mama's eyes made her wonder.

November 28, 1813. Meryton

The following morning, Darcy settled into the soft, leather covered squabs of his well-sprung coach. Soon Meryton would be but a memory and the danger to Bingley—and to his own equanimity—would be over. If Elizabeth knew what he was doing for her, she would thank him, but of course she never would. It should be enough to know himself that he was serving her.

The coach rolled past Longbourn. Would she be out walking now? He flashed a sidelong glance at the slowly passing countryside. But no light and pleasing figure rose from the grasses nor peeked out from between the trees.

Just as well.

The little pang in his belly was not disappointment. He should not have eaten those kippers before he left.

A night's sleep—helped along with a touch of laudanum— produced no improvement in Mama's humor or health. Her nerves overcame her and sent her to the refuge of her chambers. No doubt, it was her way of avoiding Mr. Collins who—despite his disappointment—could not be moved to depart any sooner than his planned date of Saturday.

At breakfast, Lydia suggested a walk into Meryton

to inquire after Mr. Wickham's return. Even if the question had not piqued her curiosity, Elizabeth would have been ready to agree simply for the pleasure of avoiding Mr. Collins.

The threat of his company at the house motivated all her sisters to join in the errand. Jane suggested adding a visit to Aunt Philips to their journey. Poor dear must be deeply troubled by the level of tension at home. She was hardly one to invent reasons to be away lest she miss a call from any of the Bingleys. Not surprisingly, Jane's suggestion met with rousing approval.

Chill November air burst against Elizabeth's face as they poured out of the front door. Cold sunshine greeted her, far more inviting than the weather when she last walked. Lydia and Kitty surged to the front, tittering among themselves, the excitement in anticipation of meeting officers clearly too much to contain. They dashed ahead, kicking up little clods of dirt and splashing in the occasional puddle as they ran. Elizabeth walked more carefully, avoiding puddles that would spoil her newly cleaned nankeen half-boots and petticoats. Such things disturbed Mama, and she was disturbed enough right now.

Elizabeth glanced over her shoulder, but the door remained closed. Mr. Collins did not appear, running to catch up with them. Was it wrong to be so relieved?

It could not be easy to be one whose absence brought greater pleasure than his presence. She should be sympathetic, but only Jane could be quite that good.

"Look! Look!" Lydia pointed at two figures stepping out of the boarding house at the edge of town.

"I think it is …" Kitty grabbed Lydia's hands.

"Mr. Wickham!" Lydia screamed and giggled.

The taller of the two figures waved energetically. That must be Denny.

Kitty and Lydia waved back, laughng. Still holding hands, they ran toward the officers, kicking up a spray of gravel in their wake.

"They should not run. It is unladylike and Mama would not approve," Mary muttered, pointedly avoiding Elizabeth's gaze.

Though she said nothing directly, there was no doubt Mary harbored many mixed and strained sentiments toward Elizabeth since Mr. Collins's proposal. Eventually they would have to talk that over, but now was not that time.

"We probably should hurry on—best not leave Kitty and Lydia unattended for too long." Jane bit her lip, staring at Kitty and Lydia.

Jane was right. They were standing too close to the officers and giggling much too freely. So close to the boarding house, they were sure to be seen by someone happy to spread gossip about them.

Mary pulled her cloak a little tighter around her shoulders and marched ahead. Jane and Elizabeth hurried to catch up.

"We were just telling Wickham how much he was missed at the Netherfield ball." Lydia looked over her shoulder and batted her eyes.

"I am humbled that my absence should have even been noticed at such a distinguished event." Wickham bowed from his shoulders.

Beside him, Denny mirrored his actions. Both men

wore their regimentals. That alone was enough to send Kitty and Lydia swooning.

"Unfortunately, business in town could not be postponed." Wickham raised his brow slightly.

Perhaps he would share the rest of that thought later.

"Business always ruins the best of our fun." Lydia pouted and sidled between the two officers. She slipped her hands into each of their arms.

Jane blushed almost the color of Lydia's scarlet cloak. "We are on our way to call upon our Aunt Philips. Perhaps you would care to join us on our call?"

Hopefully they would agree. At least that way Lydia could be ill-behaved behind closed doors instead of in the middle of the street.

Wickham and Denny exchanged a quick glance and nodded at one another.

"Mrs. Philips has extended us such warm, open hospitality already. It would be our pleasure to call upon her." Wickham's smile suggested the invitation was the highest honor he had ever been offered.

What a dramatic contrast to Mr. Collins, whose smile left her squirming, or Mr. Darcy who seemed never to smile at all.

The suggestion must have mollified Lydia. Her deportment improved to almost proper on the walk to the Philips's.

Aunt Philips was only too happy to invite them all in. A party of young people, particularly one that included eligible young men in the company of her very marriageable nieces, could not be but a delight.

They sat in her cozy—or crowded and over-decorated, depending on who was viewing it—parlor, and tea was soon brought in. Lydia and Kitty squashed up on the long sofa to sit between Wickham and Denny. Truly, Aunt Phillips should suggest that there were enough seats for everyone, but both looked so satisfied, she would have been hard pressed to move either of them. Mary sat, somewhat aloof, nearest the windows, more often looking out of them than joining in the conversation. She really was taking the turn of events with Mr. Collins very poorly. Aunt Philips hardly seemed to notice though, happily presiding over the little party from her seat near the fireplace.

"You gave us no small concern at your absence from the Netherfield ball, sir." Aunt Phillips handed Wickham a cup of tea. "We were quite relieved not to find ourselves deprived of your company, Lieutenant Denny."

"Denny is such a good dancer, is he not?" Lydia leaned close to Kitty, her tea sloshing nearly out of its cup.

Kitty launched into a painfully detailed description of the set she and Denny danced together, the one during which Mary King had stumbled.

Mr. Wickham leaned toward Elizabeth, glancing back at Lydia and Aunt Philips as though in hopes of a bit of privacy.

She cocked her head and inclined his way.

"I found as the time drew near that I had better not meet Mr. Darcy. That to be in the same room, the same party with him, for so many hours together, might be more than I could bear, and that scenes might arise unpleasant to more than myself."

"I admire your forbearance, sir, to deny yourself the very great pleasure of such an event out of consideration for the rest of the company."

His cheek dimpled with a half-smile. "I felt sure you were capable of seeing it in such light. I only hope you will not resent—"

"Mr. Darcy? Surely you cannot expect I will not harbor ill-will toward him when his very presence deprived us of your company."

"Are you speaking of the business that kept you away?" Lydia huffed. "What droll preoccupation could demand your attentions away from us?"

Wickham's eyebrow twitched, and he tipped his head toward Elizabeth. "They were very droll indeed. You could hardly take interest in my succession of busy nothings in town."

How neatly he avoided giving Lydia a direct answer. He never told an outright falsehood, distracting and side-stepping instead. Much practice must have gone into the perfecting of that skill. Jane, though, had wondered at the desirability of such a talent.

At the end of half an hour, they bid their aunt good day.

"Pray allow us to attend you home. It is much too soon to depart from such agreeable company." Wickham held the door for them as they proceeded out.

"Indeed, it is." Denny offered an arm to Kitty and the other to Lydia. With another peal of laughter they set off with him.

Mary snorted and stalked on, quickly overtaking them on the quiet roadway.

"Pray excuse me." Jane curtsied and hurried after Mary, little clouds of dust forming at her heels.

If anyone could pacify Mary's hurt feelings it was Jane.

Wickham glanced at her and slowed his pace a fraction, extending their distance from the others. "I cannot pretend to be sorry for a few moments to express my thanks for your gracious understanding, Miss Elizabeth."

"You are too kind, sir. It is you who are all gentlemanly forbearance and—"

"You think far too well of me. I am hardly a gentleman."

"Perhaps not by birth, but certainly by deportment, which is more that I can say for many who are born to the office."

"You honor me. Would that society could be so liberal-minded as well. You are most certainly an example of a true gentlewoman." How was it that his compliments always left her feeling so warm and fuzzy inside? Mr. Collins's certainly had not.

"Such flattery will certainly ruin me sir. You must be careful lest you spoil me for other company."

"Do not tell me other company fails to flatter you appropriately?"

She cocked her head and lifted her brow. "It is not seemly to flatter young women, or have you not been so told?"

"Had I been told, I would have ignored such foolishness. No accessory looks better on a young woman than a properly crafted compliment."

"My mother would agree with you, no doubt. She always approves of whoever would complement her daughters."

"A sensible woman to be sure." How did he manage such an expression of sincerity?

No one had ever said that of Mama. She pressed her lips hard not to laugh.

"May I introduce you to my parents? Mama has heard my sisters speak of you and your fellow officers so often. She has been anxious to make your acquaintance."

"I would not suppose to force a connection upon them."

"Not at all. I assure you. You are too modest. They will be most pleased of it. I would be delighted to introduce you."

"I dare not suspend any pleasure of yours. I shall be pleased for the introduction."

Hill met them at the front door. Elizabeth bid her announce their guests to her parents. Hopefully Mama would find their visit sufficient reason to leave her chambers. She had scarcely time to call for lemonade and biscuits before Mama appeared on Papa's arm at the parlor door.

Elizabeth sprang to her feet, but Lydia cut her off. "Look who we have brought to call. Lieutenant Wickham and Lieutenant Denny. We called upon Aunt Philips with them, and they walked us home."

"I am pleased to make your acquaintance." Mama curtsied.

"Indeed, sirs. The introduction is long overdue considering how your names have been attendant upon our meals these weeks now." Papa sat in his favorite wingback near the fire.

Wickham rose and bowed. "You must forgive us for intruding upon your mealtimes uninvited."

"Do not be silly, no one has been bothered by any such thing." Lydia pulled his arm. "But what does bother me is the way Elizabeth monopolizes your company. It is a bad habit on her part. Mama you really must speak to her about it."

Mama's eyes grew wide, her brows disappearing under the lace of her cap.

Papa's eyes twinkled, and he pressed his lips together. What was he thinking?

Mama stepped back and leaned out the doorway. "Hill, see refreshments are brought."

Surely Mama must know she and Jane would not neglect such basic hospitality. Elizabeth bit her lip. At least Mama was out of her rooms.

The next quarter hour passed quickly with fresh biscuits and good humor for all. The officers left Mama's improved humor in their wake, which Papa clearly approved.

"I think, Elizabeth you might have found a most singular cure to your mother's ill health. Pray it continues when Mr. Collins returns from his constitutional."

Mr. Collins's return brought back Mama's melancholy in even greater measure than before. Who would have imagined a quiet and contemplative Mr. Collins could be a trial to anyone, but he was to Mama. The letter that arrived shortly thereafter did nothing to improve Mama's spirits. Worse still, the news of the departure of Netherfield's tenants in favor of London unsettled Jane even more than Mama.

Jane felt certain it meant Mr. Bingley would never return to Meryton. How odd since Jane was usually the most positive sister among them. Truly though, he was so clearly in love with her that was hardly possible. Lizzy's firm persuasion helped her put on a brave face for their dinner at Lucas Lodge.

Though neither Mama nor Mr. Collins deigned to look at or speak to Lizzy through the whole of the evening, they both seemed in better spirits for the outing. Even better, Mr. Collins spent the better part of the next day out of the house, returning only in time for dinner.

Something had happened that day—surely it must have. He was so different during that meal, so restive, yet almost smug. At least he would be gone soon, if not for very long, for he hinted, nay threatened, to visit them ere long.

What possible purpose could he have in such designs? Elizabeth bit her knuckle and watched Mr. Collins trudge upstairs for the last time on this visit. Perhaps he might return to court Mary. That would please both Mary and Mama and resolve everything very nicely.

On that happy thought, Elizabeth retired.

November 30, 1811. Meryton

Mr. Collins took leave of them early that morning with many bows and stiffly proper words of thanks for the hospitality shown him by Longbourn. Mama's eyes brimmed, and her hands fluttered as she stammered encouragement for him to return soon, even going so far as to imply he should have hopes for a material change to have taken place in the hearts and minds of Longbourn when he returned. Odd, how he simply seemed to ignore that remark. It should have been pleasing that he did so, but instead it was rather ominous.

How pleasant was breakfast without the threat of

Mr. Collins making an appearance and interrupting their conversations with remarks on Lady Catherine's opinions; the grandeur of Rosings Park; or the comments of sermon writers on the proper behavior of young ladies.

Even better, Charlotte arrived shortly thereafter, ready for conversation. How strange, though, that she did not bring a work basket with her. Something about the crease in her brow, the way she carried her shoulders, something was definitely wrong.

"Would it be possible for us to speak alone for a few moments, in privacy?" Charlotte asked.

"Of course, perhaps a turn about the garden?" Elizabeth ushered her outside.

They blinked in the bright morning sun. The mild warmth of the day was just beginning to break the early chill left over from the previous evening. They headed toward the little wilderness. Charlotte was not much of a walker, and the trees, even though they were mostly brown and bare, would offer a degree of privacy without taxing her endurance too much. Many steps passed in silence.

"I can see something troubles you. Is everything well with your family?" Elizabeth bit her lip and steeled herself for bad news. Was Sir William ill?

Their skirts rustled against drying leaves, and small twigs snapped underfoot.

"Yes, yes, very well—quite well in fact. I fear though, I have some news that you may find disagreeable." Charlotte wrung her hands, twisting her tan kid gloves as she did. If she continued, she might well ruin them.

"Best tell me quickly then, and preserve me from fretting over the nature of it." Pray not let her say the thing Elizabeth had snickered about to herself before drifting to sleep last night.

"I know you will find this difficult to conceive." Charlotte stopped and looked Elizabeth full in the face. "I am engaged to your cousin."

"That is not possible!" That was probably not the correct thing to say.

"It is quite possible and entirely true. He came to me yesterday with an offer of marriage, which I have accepted."

"But it was only just on Wednesday—" Elizabeth covered her mouth with her hand.

"That he made an offer to you. I am well aware. He made no secret of that to me." Charlotte smiled a tight smile.

"You do not find it alarming he made a similar offer to you but two days later?"

"I have dwelt upon that truth, but I am satisfied in his explanation of being able to seemingly switch his allegiances so easily."

"There is nothing seeming about it, it is exactly what he has done. Forgive me, my friend, but I am astonished at your having accepted him."

Charlotte turned her head—probably so Elizabeth could not see her roll her eyes—and began walking again. "Why should you be surprised my dear Eliza? Do you think it incredible that Mr. Collins should be able to procure any woman's good opinion because he was not so happy to succeed with you?"

In truth, the answer was a thousand times yes. No woman with any sense or dignity could accept such a man as he.

"I can see what you are feeling. But when you have had time to think it over, I hope you will be satisfied with what I have done." Charlotte wrapped her arms around her waist. "I am not romantic, you know. I never was. I ask only a comfortable home, and considering Mr. Collins's character, connections, and situation in life, I am convinced that my chance of happiness with him is as fair as most people can boast on entering the marriage state." Charlotte turned back toward Longbourn house.

"Undoubtedly," Elizabeth whispered, not that she meant it, but it was a polite thing to say.

What a dreadful opinion Charlotte must have of marriage altogether. All this time, they had apparently not shared the idea it should be a bond built on mutual affection. To see Charlotte accept a man for no reason but worldly gain—did she even know her friend at all?

She squeezed her eyes shut, but the image of Charlotte in a matron's cap beside Mr. Collins, with a line of children all looking like him impinged upon her. Could a comfortable home truly balance the daily humiliations of being attached to such a man? Did Charlotte have any real idea of what she had done?

Their walk back to the house was quiet save for the crisp leaves under their half-boots and a distant bird calling out its loneliness to any who would listen. Charlotte quickly took her leave, probably sensing rightly Elizabeth required time to ponder the unexpected turn of events.

How much time would it require to reconcile such an unfathomable decision? Would she ever be able to see Charlotte in a favorable light again?

Elizabeth took a slow turn about the garden alone, but no answers lurked among the autumn hollyhocks and gillyflowers. So, she brought her work basket into the parlor and joined Mama and her sisters. Mama sat in her favorite chair near the fireplace, pretending to sew whilst she regularly glanced at Elizabeth and sighed. Jane sat at the writing desk at the far side of the room pretending to write a letter. Mary stared at the same page of her book for no less than ten minutes pretending to read. Kitty and Lydia, though, were in better spirits, playing a board game at the table near the window.

Lydia talked more than played—enough words for two, maybe three young ladies. Hopefully that meant Elizabeth would not be called upon for some meaningful contribution to the conversation.

Pray let them not ask after Charlotte! What would she tell Mama? Should she say anything at all? Charlotte had not given her leave to share the news.

Hill appeared in the doorway. "Sir William Lucas, madam."

Mama muttered and groaned, heaving herself to her feet. "Show him in."

"Greetings and felicitations to you, Mrs. Bennet." Sir William trundled in and bowed. "And Miss Bennet, Miss Elizabeth, Miss Mary, Miss Kitty and Miss Lydia. I come at the behest of my daughter, bearing great good news."

Elizabeth grimaced; her stomach clenched. No! Not Sir William! Who was more perfectly crafted to agitate Mama with such news as he had to express? She cast about the room; there must be some way to stop him.

"Any good news for your family will be most welcome intelligence." Mama's voice turned brittle as the color left her face. "Do come in and allow us to share in your celebration."

He opened his hands as if to display a treasure. "My dear Charlotte has charged me to bring you the news of her betrothal."

"Betrothal?" Mama choked on the word and grabbed for the back of her chair.

Lydia looked at him over her shoulder and laughed. "Charlotte is engaged? To whom?"

"Please forgive my sister. We had no idea anyone was calling upon Charlotte." Jane shot a bug-eyed glare at Lydia.

"I take no offense, none at all. It all came together most suddenly—entirely unexpectedly." Sir William's smile was decidedly … polite.

"To whom is she betrothed?" Mama forced the words through gritted teeth.

"Why to your cousin, Mr. Collins, good madam."

Mary snapped her book shut, pallor creeping over her face.

"Mr. Collins?" Mama's voice tightened to a shriek, and she threw her head back, laughing. "I never took you as one for a humbug, Sir William, but you certainly have crafted a fine one."

His eyes widened, and he took half a step back. Whatever reaction he had expected, this certainly was not among the possibilities. A full minute passed before he regained his power of speech. "Pray no, madam, there is no humbug at all. My news is entirely factual. Charlotte is betrothed to Mr. Collins."

"That is simply not possible. He made an offer to my Elizabeth not three days ago. He could not possibly have made an offer to anyone else, much less your daughter, in so short a time." Mama held her left hand behind her back and balled it into a fist.

How did he manage to contain his reactions and

continue to be so polite? He continued to smile and insist, but Mama would hear nothing of it.

Elizabeth wrung her hands. "Mama, please, Sir William speaks the truth."

Mama whirled on her. "What do you know of this?"

"Charlotte came to see me this morning. She ... she told me Mr. Collins made her an offer, and she accepted. Sir William is not at all mistaken."

"That cannot be. You ... you are to be married to him ... not ... not ..." she waved a pointing finger toward Sir William.

Jane jumped to her feet and steadied Mama. "Please convey our best wishes and happiness to Charlotte and Lady Lucas. We ... all of us ... wish her joy."

He dabbed his forehead with his handkerchief and bowed deeply. "Thank you, Miss Bennet."

"Indeed," Elizabeth stood, "we are very pleased for her and for Mr. Collins."

"How can you say such a thing, Lizzy? Do not presume to speak for me. This is surely a mistake, and I cannot rejoice in it at all." Mama shuffled from one foot to the other like an uneasy hen.

Sir William mopped his forehead again and slipped half a step back. "Forgive me, madam, but I am very sure of the discussion I had with the gentleman in question. He goes to Kent to prepare settlement papers directly."

"Pray, Mama—" Lizzy sent her a pleading look.

"Mind yourself, Miss Lizzy. I told you I would never see you again, and I have little desire to see you or anyone now. Excuse me, Sir William, I am most unwell." She flounced from the room, leaving a wake of gaping jaws behind her.

"Pray excuse our mother," Jane stammered. Clearly she was searching for some way to cover Mama's rudeness, but even a saint would find it difficult to create a plausible excuse.

"Do not worry, Miss Bennet. I know her delicate constitution makes it difficult for her to bear with unexpected news. Fear not, I am quite certain no offense is meant, and none is taken. If you will excuse me though, I have several other calls to make this morning on my daughter's behalf." He bowed and showed himself out.

Jane shut the door and stared at Elizabeth.

"Charlotte Lucas engaged to Mr. Collins?" Lydia bounced up from her seat and bobbed in front of Elizabeth. "How could you keep such delicious news to yourself? You are quite horrible keeping it secret."

"Delicious news?" Mary's voice broke. "I think it as terrible as Mama." She threw her book on her chair and fled the room.

No doubt she would consider herself quite jilted and lovelorn now, though Mr. Collins had paid her no special regard.

Heavens, that was an ungracious thought!

"Perhaps we should go to Mama." Jane bit her lip.

Hill appeared. "The missus calls for Miss Elizabeth."

"See to Mary, I am sure she will need your comfort." Elizabeth whispered as she passed Jane.

"She is in her chambers." Hill tried to smile, but the effect was more of a grimace.

Just the place for another delightful chorus of "How could you refuse Mr. Collins?" A delightful and charming way to spend the afternoon. She dragged her feet as long as she could, but eventually she arrived at her mother's door, conveniently left open for her.

"Come in, and close the door." Mama's voice was thin and sharp as a winter wind. "Come to me. Do not hover near the door. I have no intention of shouting." Whatever her intentions, there was little doubt this conversation would involve shouting at some point.

All the curtains were drawn, throwing the cluttered room into deep shadows. The bed and chairs were piled high with pillows; the press and small tables held bric-a-brac enough to keep the maids dusting for a lifetime. A bowl of dried roses fragranced the room with a dry, dusty sort of perfume that somehow felt very old.

"So it is true, Charlotte is to be married to Mr. Collins?" Mama beckoned in short, angry motions.

Elizabeth inched closer into the deep shadows. "That is what Charlotte told me. I have no reason to disbelieve her."

"Then he is entirely lost to you girls."

"It would seem to be the case."

"I hope you understand what you have done, Elizabeth." Mama's cold flat voice chilled her more deeply than a snowstorm.

She pulled her shoulders back and clasped her hands behind her back "I refused a hopelessly unsuitable match."

"How sharper than a serpent's tooth it is to have a thankless child! We will all be in the hedgerows because of you." Mama pointed at her, hand shaking.

"I hardly think—"

"Indeed, indeed, you do not consider anyone but yourself. You seek only your pleasure for today without regard for the situations of others and for the reality of their future. I am heartily ashamed of you. Ashamed."

She said the word so easily. Had she any notion of how deeply it cut?

"You shirk your duty to all of us and for what? For what? I do not understand."

Elizabeth swallowed hard, blinking rapidly to ease her burning eyes. "If you do not understand, then I cannot possibly explain it to you."

"Do not be snippy with me, Miss Lizzy. When I was your age, I knew my duty, and I did it by becoming Mrs. Bennet as soon as I possibly could. I have never regretted it, at least not until today, as I am forced to look upon the cake you have made of everything. How are we to live when your father is dead? Answer me that!"

"Does Jane not have hopes yet for Mr. Bingley?"

"She does, she does indeed, but hopes are only that until the settlements are signed and the marriage is done. I hope she will marry him. I expect she will marry him," Mama covered the distance between them in two brisk steps and poked Elizabeth's chest. "But it was you who were made an offer and refused it. What is to become of us! What I ask you!"

There was little point in trying to answer such a question.

"I will tell you this. If it were not for the officers you brought home yesterday, I would indeed never see you again."

At this moment that possibility sounded rather pleasing.

"I hope that effort was you repenting of your error and trying to make amends for it. I still do not know if I will accept your energies, though. Perhaps now, you can see how very great your foolishness is."

Elizabeth held her breath. She dared not risk speaking her mind now.

"That Wickham fellow seems quite charming enough for all your foolish romantical notions. And he is an officer. I fully expect to see you behave in a more fitting way with him than you did with Mr. Collins. Go now and fetch Hill for me. My nerves! Oh, my poor nerves!"

Elizabeth scurried out, instructed Hill and bolted outside.

Fresh air, she needed fresh air, although even that was tainted with the memory of her recent assignation with Charlotte. The garden would not do. The footpath toward Oakum Mount, that was a far better plan.

Soon the shade of the path closed in over her and the cool spread over her heated spirits.

Had Mama just ordered her to flirt with Mr. Wickham? How else was she to interpret Mama's command? There was no way around it, Mama had suggested she secure Mr. Wickham as soon as may be possible just as Charlotte had suggested Jane should secure Mr. Bingley.

Elizabeth caught herself against a large oak and clutched it for support. It did not seem it mattered to Mama whom she married, so long as she did it quickly.

At least Mr. Wickham was a much more agreeable conquest than Mr. Collins could ever be. He was warm and open and easy company. He had an excellent sense of humor, was well-spoken and a very good dancer. Though he had a sad history with Mr. Darcy, he did have a great many friends around him. By all accounts, he was a very eligible man.

Eligible and agreeable—that seemed a rare combination.

Perhaps it would not be a bad thing to become further acquainted. At least it would please Mama. Certainly she would not throw herself at him, that would be unseemly at best and entirely beyond her nature. But she would not mind getting to know him better.

In fact, that might be a very pleasing thing indeed.

.

❧Chapter 3

December 6, 1811 St. Nicholas' day. London

JUST OVER A se'nnight later, Darcy stepped out of his solicitor's office onto the largely barren street and adjusted the capes on his greatcoat against the sharp breeze and grey looming skies. It was unfortunate Mr. Rushout could no longer continue in his office as Pemberley's steward. Fortunately, the solicitor knew of some promising candidates. But reviewing their letters of introduction would take some time and meeting with them would take even more. With any luck the process could be completed by spring.

That meant he would have to supervise the spring planting more closely than usual, but perhaps that was not a bad thing either. A man should never get too far from the business of his land. He patted his portfolio, stuffed with letters and papers to review.

Deep thunder rattled the nearby windows, and a chill blast of wind, tinged with the scent of impending rain, tore past. The downpour would not hold off until he reached Darcy House. But there was a coffee house—Blair's—just two streets away. If he hurried, he might make it there before the storm.

Fat raindrops pelted him the last half dozen steps to the coffee house, but he ducked inside just before the pounding rains unleashed. A serving girl saw him to a table in an isolated corner and took his order. He sat with his back to the wall and glanced about the room.

The place smelt a bit dank, but that may have just been an artifact of the weather. On the whole it was probably cleaner than most such establishments. The table was covered with a clean cloth and it seemed the floor had recently been swept; all details in its favor, even if the furnishings were mismatched and somewhat dingy, a little like the clientele. Still, the other customers appeared gentlemanly enough to make this a tolerable enough stop.

Appealing aromas drifted from the kitchen, baked goods, soup or stew perhaps, and the strong scent of fresh coffee. The serving girl returned with a pot of coffee and a platter of cold meat and bread. A bit of nuncheon would help distract him from the tedium of the task at hand. He broke the seal on the first letter of introduction, a Mr. Northwick. Studied at Eton and Cambridge …

"Darcy!"

He started and looked up, directly into Bingley's grinning face.

"Fancy meeting you here. I had no idea you frequented Blair's too!" Bingley pulled out a chair and sat down.

"I have never been here before. It seemed an expedient location to avoid the rain."

"An expedient location to avoid the rain? Seriously, Darcy?" Bingley laughed heartily, cheeks glowing whether from the chill outside or his mirth, Darcy could not tell. "At least you are enjoying some of their very fine coffee. You must have some Sally Lunn bread. It really is not to be missed." He waved the serving girl over and requested some, along with a pot of tea.

That was Bingley. He had a way of just marching into one's quiet life and injecting his own brand of marginally controlled mayhem into it.

"I am glad to see you. Very glad. Caroline has an invitation she wants me to convey."

"Caroline? I thought we had discussed the matter already, and you know my thoughts quite clearly."

"Pish posh, Darcy you are jumping to conclusions. Caroline is hosting a Christmas dinner at Grosvenor Street and wishes to include you amongst the guests."

"You know I do not prefer to socialize. It would be best for me to abstain."

"You ought not spend Christmas alone. That is far too lonely a fate for a man with both friends and family. Besides, this party is your fault." Something in Bingley's tone—a party being someone's fault? That was a sentiment quite unlike him.

"My fault? That is absurd."

Bingley raised his index finger and shook it at him. "I would not be here in London, apart from your forceful insistence that it was the right and proper thing to do. Were I not in London, this party would not be happening. Thus, since it is your fault I am in London, the party is equally your responsibility. As such, you must attend."

Darcy huffed and pinched the bridge of his nose. It almost sounded as though Bingley did not enjoy being in London. But that was hardly possible. He always enjoyed town.

"Surely you cannot tell me you object to Christmastide entertaining?" Bingley drummed his fingers on the table.

Though he was not apt to socialize, he did not on principle object to Christmastide socializing. This year was different, though. If only he might be left alone, he might quiet the cacophony in his own head. One which centered on Miss Elizabeth Bennet.

He squeezed his eyes shut and shook his head sharply. Why was it, the very thing he least wanted to dwell upon would not leave his mind for a king's ransom? Perhaps distraction among merry society was the best thing indeed. "No, I do not object. You may thank your sister for her gracious invitation, and tell her I will be there."

"Capital! Absolutely capital! She will be very pleased." The serving girl dropped a plate of warm Sally Lunn bread on the table between them. "Now, we must enjoy some of this bread before it gets cold. You will not regret it."

"The party or the bread?"

"Neither one!"

Bingley was correct on one count; the bread was excellent. As to the other, it would remain to be seen.

The rain dwindled to a tolerable drizzle, and Darcy offered his take leave, tucking his neglected paperwork back into his portfolio. Bingley could be a bit of a rattle at times, but sometimes the distraction was pleasing, even if it meant he now had a social obligation for a Christmas dinner. Wearisome as it might be, Bingley was probably right, it was better than spending the evening alone.

Even with just sprinkles and mist, the rain left him feeling damp and vaguely cold by the time he reached Darcy House. Leaving his greatcoat with the housekeeper to be properly dried, he bypassed his study and went directly to his room for dry clothes, his favorite banyan, and a warm fire. He settled into his favorite overstuffed leather chair and propped his feet up.

The room was quiet save the fire's crackling. Shadows danced along the walls' walnut paneling. Deep green wool drapes were pulled shut against the chill. Snug and warm and private, if a little lonely.

Though he had not asked for it, the housekeeper sent up a mug of hot cider which accompanied a small package on a silver tray. What was that? He picked it up, revealing a note bearing his name in a very familiar handwriting.

Georgiana.

He leaned back and smiled. She had remembered. That probably should not please him so much as it did, but there it was.

He opened the note.

My dear brother,

I am sorry we could not be together this St. Nicholas' Day, but I find I enjoy our tradition far too much to allow distance to stand in the way. I hope this finds you well and warm, and that you will think of me when you use it.

GD

He chuckled softly. In some ways they were so alike. He had sent a similar note and package to Pemberley with instructions to Mrs. Reynolds to make sure Georgiana had it today. Hopefully she would enjoy the new sheet music—perhaps she might even play for him when he returned. She was still so shy after all that had happened. Would that ever change? What would it take to see her back to her cheerful, albeit quiet self?

He opened the brown paper wrapping revealing three embroidered linen handkerchiefs, one with his initials in white silk, one with a fine pulled-thread design, and the last with a sprig of lavender. What an odd choice.

Miss Elizabeth always smelt like lavender. No doubt it would be one of her favorite flowers. She would appreciate Georgiana's fine sewing and her thoughtful generous nature. Miss Elizabeth would probably be good for Georgiana, helping her find laughter and confidence once again.

What would Elizabeth think of the Darcy family tradition of St. Nicholas Day gifts? Would she find it frivolous or old fashioned, or just too sentimental? No, she seemed far more sympathetic than that. What family traditions did the Bennets observe during the Christmastide season? What would it be like merging traditions from two families? Would it be difficult to embrace different customs even as he would want her to embrace his?

He threw his head back and groaned. Why should the Bennets' Christmastide practices matter to him? And why did she continue to come, unbidden into his thoughts?

December 16, 1811 Meryton

Over the next fortnight, neighborhood dinners and parties offered numerous opportunities for contact with Mr. Wickham. Enough so, Mama's ill-temper and health were largely unchanged. For the time being at least, little, if anything could make up for Elizabeth's refusal of Mr. Collins and Charlotte's victory, but her continued interaction with—and encouragement of—Mr. Wickham helped.

The effect did not survive the return of Mr. Collins, though. Mama took to her rooms, complaining loudly of the inconvenience of having him at Longbourn when by all rights he should stay at Lucas Lodge, especially when her health remained so indifferent.

As if young men were not vexing enough, Mr. Bingley's continued absence did little to improve matters. The gossips of Meryton now circulated the intelligence that Mr. Bingley meant to quit Netherfield for the whole of the winter.

That was probably due to the successful efforts of Mr. Bingley's sisters. No doubt they wished to keep him away. The efforts of the two unfeeling women, and his overpowering friend, Mr. Darcy, assisted by the attractions of Miss Darcy—was she even actually in London?—and the amusements of London, were likely strong enough to overwhelm his attachments to Jane.

Poor Jane so suffered under the anxiety of the situation. They could never speak of the matter between them, though; it was too much for Jane to bring to words, so she suffered in silence.

Mama, though, enjoyed no such delicate restraint and plagued them constantly with her complaints over it all when she was not describing her abhorrence of Charlotte Lucas as her successor as Longbourn's mistress. Poor Jane began keeping to her room.

Two days later, a letter from Miss Bingley arrived. Jane said little and pointedly avoided Mama and anyone else who might question her as to its contents.

The following morning, she bade Elizabeth to her room and showed her the letter. Elizabeth curled up on Jane's neatly made bed as Jane paced along the short wall by the window, dodging the press and the dressing table that blocked her path.

Miss Bingley neatly described their enjoyment in London, Mr. Bingley's partiality to Miss Darcy, and her expectations for its right and natural conclusions. How like her to put an end to all doubt of Mr. Bingley's plans and attachments.

Though Jane readily believed the letter, it was difficult not to wonder just how much of it was the truth of Mr. Bingley's state, and how much was wishful thinking on the part of Miss Bingley. She was the type of person who would assert how she hoped things would be rather than how they actually were.

Jane paced along the long wall now, in front of the fireplace, the mantle stained with smoke. "If Mr. Bingley's sisters believed him attached to me, they would not try to part us. They are not so unkind. Moreover, if he were so attached, they could not succeed in parting us."

Elizabeth pulled her knees up under her chin. "I

fear you credit his sisters with far more good will than I believe them capable of."

Jane sank down in the window seat. The sunlight behind her glowed like a halo. "By supposing Mr. Bingley's affection toward me, you make everybody act unnaturally and wrong, and me most unhappy. I pray you, do not distress me by the idea." She ran her long fingers down the edge of the curtain. "I am not ashamed of having been mistaken. At least it is slight and nothing in comparison of what I should feel in thinking ill of him or his sisters. Let me take it in the best light in which it may be understood."

How could she directly oppose such a wish? Best refrain from mentioning Mr. Bingley's name to Jane again.

Forbearance though did not prevent her from thinking about the matter at great length. If Jane was correct and her separation from Mr. Bingley was to be permanent, then Mama's anxiety was … heavens it was not nearly so groundless as it had seemed earlier. With none of the Bennet sisters enjoying any prospects for marriage, their situation, should tragedy befall them, looked bleak indeed.

Though not formed for melancholy, the thought did give Elizabeth great pause.

December 18, 1811. London

Darcy dismissed his valet and took a final glance in the mirror. Well-brushed black coat, crisp white cravat, shoes polished to a shine. He was neat, proper, and hopefully unremarkable. Though it was only a small card party at the Matlocks', it would be his luck to encounter some gossip writer skulking around the nearby streets, like a weasel waiting to sneak into the henhouse. Scavengers and vermin, all of them. The back of his neck twitched.

Card play was hardly amusing. If he had any choice in the matter, he would skip the whole thing. But that would offend Aunt and Uncle Matlock, a greater price than he was ready to pay for the luxury of an evening at home.

He went to his study to get in a few minutes of work before the coach was ready. A recent letter from Mr. Rushout required his attention. Just as he settled down to read it, the housekeeper peeked in and rapped on the doorframe. He waved her in.

She curtsied in front of his desk. A small, somewhat severe-looking woman with dark hair and darker eyes, her size was deceptive. She had a sharp, quick mind and could recall the tiniest detail about anything related to her work. Darcy House had been without a mistress since Mother had died, but despite that lack of guidance, she ran the house flawlessly.

"Sir, it is coming up on St. Thomas's Day. Have you any special instructions about the mumpers this year?"

Not something he had given any thought to at all. "Are there many of them?"

"We have a fair number who visit each year, and what with all the losses to the French, the numbers have only grown."

Unfortunately, she was right. Napoleon had ensured England would not run short of widows.

"In the past, we have always had wheat for them, sir."

Darcy chewed his lower lip. "Do that, and give them a few pennies as well."

"That is very generous of you, sir." Though she would never say such a thing, something in her eyes looked pleased.

"In these cases, I think it better to do too much than too little, do you not?"

"I know they will be very grateful." She curtsied again and left as the footman appeared to announce the carriage.

He settled into the soft leather carriage squabs. The smell of fresh polish lingered in the air, a bit too strong for his liking. So, he pulled open the curtains and the side glass for a bit of fresh air.

The streets were crowded this evening and the going slow enough that Darcy could clearly see the faces of those they passed. So many people!

Peddlers, their faces dusty and worn, calling out their wares with heavy packs on their backs or loaded hand carts. Tradesmen making deliveries, boxes piled high. The occasional dandy and his mates, parading around, hoping for notice. And the beggars.

They were everywhere, paupers, begging for help and sustenance. It was difficult to tell the deserving from the undeserving poor. How many times had he been counseled to give only to the deserving poor? But how was one to know who was truly deserving?

A woman, worn and tattered, with two young children in tow looked at him with hollow eyes. Her face was dirty, and so very, very tired. She was young for a widow. Probably a soldier's wife. He waved at her with one hand and reached into his pocket with the other. She limped as she hurried toward his carriage, sending one of the children, a young boy ahead of her. Darcy tossed him a coin before the carriage was out of reach and the child ran it back to his mother. Tears ran down her face as she waved her thanks.

He leaned back and closed his eyes. How many young girls chased after a smart uniform? Certainly, the young women in Meryton had. What would they do if they encountered real officers like Fitzwilliam, not mere militia? Would Miss Elizabeth consider marrying a soldier? Her mother certainly would not warn her against it.

If she did, how easily could she end up as that poor wretch in the streets? He gulped, stomach knotted. Far, far too easily, and through no fault of her own. Surely, her family though, they would take care of her, would they not? If her father were alive, there was no question, but if Collins was master of Longbourn—with his own self-righteousness and Aunt Catherine's judgmental nature, charity would be hard to find from his household.

He scrubbed his eyes with his palm, but still the image of that woman remained. That was too cruel a fate for a woman like Miss Elizabeth. But what could he do about it?

Nothing, absolutely nothing.

Tomorrow he would instruct the housekeeper to increase what was set aside for the mumpers.

December 19, 1811. Meryton

The following evening, Lady Lucas hosted a party to celebrate Charlotte's upcoming nuptials. Elizabeth, Kitty, and Lydia waited in the front hall, buttoning their redingotes and adjusting their muffs. Lydia and

Kitty giggled still over the thought of anyone actually marrying Mr. Collins.

Mama declared herself far too ill to attend. She went so far as to suggest that the weather might be too disagreeable for frivolous travel and the rest of the family might remain at home as well.

"My dear Mrs. Bennet," Papa slipped on his great coat in the crowded vestibule, "I have seen you traverse the countryside in foul weather for a bit of gossip following an assembly. A few rainy clouds will not keep us from doing our duty by our neighbors."

Mama stood at the top of the stairs in her dressing gown, waving her handkerchief before her face. "I think it very cruel that you would deprive me of all my daughters' company when I am so very unwell. I could die before you return, then how would you feel?"

"I doubt your nerves will be the source of a sudden demise over the course of a single evening." Papa muttered something else under his breath, but best not try to make it out.

"Perhaps it would be aapropriate to allow Mary to stay with her." Jane appeared from behind Mama's shoulder and raised her eyebrow at Elizabeth.

Mary was taking Mr. Collins's visit very hard indeed. Although she complained far less than Mama, her suffering was probably more real. Forcing on her an evening spent in Charlotte's presence would be truly cruel.

"I think Jane's idea a good one," Elizabeth whispered, straightening the capes across Papa's shoulders.

He huffed. "Very well, Mary, you may stay behind and tend to your mother, if you wish."

"Yes, Papa," Mary called from somewhere upstairs.

Jane took Mama's elbow and led her back toward her chambers.

"Well, I dare say that will make the ride to the Lucas's much more agreeable. I hate being squashed up in the carriage so." Lydia peered into the vestibule's mirror and pulled a curl out from under her bonnet.

"I am more thankful that Mr. Collins is already there, and we do not have to ride with him." Kitty giggled.

Papa rolled his eyes. "Come, come, the carriage is waiting, unless of course you prefer to walk."

"I am here, Papa." Jane hurried down the steps and followed them out to the carriage.

The driver handed them up into the coach and they settled into the worn, cracked leather seats. Some warm bricks would have been nice, but no one had thought to ask for them, so they would just have to make do without. Still, Lydia was right; the ride was far more comfortable with two fewer ladies in the coach. Roomier and far easier on Elizabeth's equanimity. It was one thing to endure Mama's open rudeness to the Lucases in the privacy of their own home, but far different to anticipate witnessing it publicly. Perhaps that was why Papa permitted her to stay at home.

"Lizzy, Lizzy!" Lydia kicked her shin. "Pay attention, I am talking to you."

"Pray stop that." Elizabeth rubbed her shin. At least Lydia had not left a mark on her dress.

"I heard that the officers and Colonel Forster were invited to the party tonight. I expect they shall all be there. I want to dance and converse with all of them."

"And why are you taking particular pains to tell me something so obvious?" Elizabeth bit her tongue. She really did need to moderate her sharp tone.

"Because every time we have seen him recently, you have hogged Mr. Wickham's attention for yourself. We have all noticed. It is time for you to stop. You must share him with the rest of us."

Elizabeth's cheeks burned. Had anyone else perceived her spending so much time in his company? Even if they had, was it truly such a bad thing? He was so very agreeable, and seemed equally pleased with her.

"Lydia, do not be so unkind. Lizzy has done nothing of the sort and you know it. You are just jealous that you must share the officers' attention with anyone else." Jane's lips pursed into the nearest expression to a frown she could muster.

"That is not true! Have you seen the way she talks with him, keeping the rest of us away with her complicated conversation and—"

"Enough." Papa brought his heel down sharply. "Fuss all you like about the attentions of young men. But when you impugn sensible conversation, I have had quite enough of it."

Elizabeth leaned back into the squabs. At least Jane did not think her behavior distasteful. Nor did Papa, or he would have joined in the teasing. She could anticipate Mr. Wickham's congenial company with a clear conscience.

Sir William himself greeted them at the door. They employed a housekeeper who was perfectly well able to perform the office, but whenever they entertained, he insisted on being the first face his guests would see. Charlotte had once confided that he thought it made him appear more affable.

Would they ever share such confidences again? It was difficult to see how.

"Mrs. Bennet is not with you tonight?" Sir William bowed deeply and waved a maid to take their wraps.

"I am afraid Mama is unwell this evening." Jane's smile, though pretty enough, felt faded and worn. "Our sister Mary has stayed behind to tend her. They both send their regrets tonight."

"They shall both be greatly missed." Sir William was a very bad liar. The unmitigated relief in his eyes betrayed him as surely as if he wore a sign around his neck.

Who could blame him though? Neither Mama nor Mary was by any means subtle about their feelings. It was to his credit that he would have invited them at all.

"Eliza!" Charlotte appeared at her father's shoulder and grasped Elizabeth's hands. "How very glad I am to see you tonight."

"I would not dream of missing this." Hopefully she was not as bad a liar as Sir William.

Watching others congratulate Charlotte on what surely must be a decision that would bring her unhappiness would be difficult at best. But there were things that one did to honor a friendship.

"Come in. I think there is company here you will find agreeable." Charlotte looped her arm in Elizabeth's and edged her way around the crowded room.

What space was not taken up by old, somewhat worn furniture was filled by people. Sir William always managed to invite more people than his house would comfortably hold. There was always greater than average risk of someone knocking over a candle-stick with so many elbows and shoulders in play.

"Miss Elizabeth." Mr. Wickham sauntered—or more rightly sidled— toward them, flanked by two other officers. "How welcome to see you here to-night."

"Thank you very much. My younger sisters are here as well." She inclined her head toward Kitty and Lydia at the opposite side of the room.

Mr. Wickham's companions abandoned him in favor of the small flock of young ladies.

"Excuse me, Eliza, Papa is calling to me." Charlotte dipped in a tiny curtsey and wove her way toward the vestibule.

"There was some talk that you might not be here tonight." The corner of Mr. Wickham's mouth turned up a bit.

"Indeed? Why ever would that be?"

"Perhaps I should not be the bearer of such news. Word has it that Miss Lucas was not the first recipient of Mr. Collins's … attentions. One might think that to be in the same party with her for so many hours together, could be more than you could bear. I would certainly not blame you at all if that were the case."

Elizabeth gasped and pressed her hands to her cheeks. Every servant in Longbourn village, and consequently in Meryton, must have heard the story by now. Why had Mama not learned to keep her peace?

"Forgive me. I fear I have embarrassed you." Mr. Wickham peered at her closely.

"I hardly know what to say. I had not considered that it would be widely known. I bear no ill-will to-ward my friend and am perfectly content to be in her company. It is entirely disquieting to think that anyone should believe otherwise."

"I would not be concerned if I were you. You are here and that disproves any rumored animosity between you and your friend. Your reputation as one of the kindest ladies in Meryton is quite safe." He leaned a modicum closer and whispered, "Moreover, the fact you were his first choice shows his good taste, and the fact that he is now with his second choice shows yours."

Elizabeth fought back a snicker.

"That is much better. Good humor becomes you."

"Thank you, sir. I shall try to remember that."

"Your admirers would all prefer to see you thus." His eye twitched in what surely must have been a wink.

"Now you flatter me. I would have thought you would know better than to offer such idle flattery to a young woman."

"It is hardly idle." Gracious, how his eyes sparkled in the candle light. The dimples in his cheeks were so very, very appealing. "If you will not allow me to speak of your charms, then perhaps I might be indulged a question."

"Perhaps, sir. But I know you too well to permit you *carte blanche* in such a matter." Her heart beat just a mite harder and faster.

"You wound me!"

"With my rapier wit?"

He chuckled. "I know your family were on rather intimate terms with the Bingleys. Have you any idea regarding their return to Netherfield?"

A chill snaked down her back.

"Forgive me, I have offended."

"Not you, sir, not you." She bit her lip and looked at the soot stained ceiling. "Though we had hoped otherwise, it now appears that the Bingleys are engaged in town for the remainder of the winter. It seems we shall not be enjoying their society any time soon."

"I am very sorry to hear that. I know his company was particularly agreeable to your sister."

"His company shall be missed."

"But not his sisters'." His lip curled back just a mite. "No, you did not by any means say that. I speak for myself. They both were far too much like Mr. Darcy for my liking."

"Indeed, they are. At least Mr. Darcy's company shall not be a burden this winter." She bit her tongue. It would not do to share the contents of Jane's post with him.

"Always one to look on the bright side. He was not one of the countryside's chiefest charms."

"So, you find our county charming, sir? What do you pronounce its best feature?"

He looked out over the crowded, noisy room. "Without a doubt, the company. I have hardly found a place more welcoming. You know the militia often meets with less friendly hosts. I have marveled at how agreeable Meryton and Hertfordshire have been. I must thank you, for you and your family have been a great part of that. Your parents' approbation has certainly influenced the opinion of the rest of the community."

"You impart a great deal of influence to my family. Perhaps you think too well of us, but it is a vice I can easily overlook."

Oh, the way he smiled! No wonder Lydia yearned for his attentions.

"I pray all my vices are so easy to overlook." He clasped his hands behind his back.

"Have you many of them?"

"I fear there are far more than you have noted."

"I shall be more careful in my observations then."

He stepped half a step closer and met her gaze. His eyes were so warm and sincere, full of ... of something she could not name. "I should very much enjoy being the object of your close study."

Surely there must be some appropriate response, but none availed itself, so she stood gaping at him.

"You are doing it again!" Lydia stomped and crossed her arms, wedging herself between Elizabeth and Wickham.

"Lydia!" Elizabeth jumped back.

"Shall I not have my share of the conversation?" Lydia smiled up at Mr. Wickham, batting her eyes.

Wickham winked at Elizabeth. "Of course you shall." He offered his arm. "I see a young lady I do not know. Will you introduce me?"

"That awful freckled thing? That is just Mary King. I cannot imagine why you would want to know her."

"Nonetheless, it is right for us to be introduced, and who better to do the honors than you?"

"Oh, very well." Lydia clung to Wickham's arm. "You will see she is dull indeed and not worth knowing at all. Come along."

Lydia pulled Wickham away, with a quick wrinkled-nose backward glance.

The impertinence might have upset her except Wickham followed with a long-suffering look of his own.

It was a shame to lose his company, but perhaps it was best not to spend the entire evening in conversation with him to the exclusion of others. Surely there would be the opportunity to enjoy more of his society later.

.

✤ Chapter 4

December 20, 1811 Meryton

THE NEXT MORNING, Mr. Collins left Long-bourn very early—probably planning to partake of his breakfast at Lucas Lodge. Elizabeth took her accustomed place at the round table, near the windows. How pleasant it was not to have Mr. Collins crowding her elbow. With only Jane sitting directly beside her, the normally cozy blue and white room felt positively spacious.

Racks of toast, preserves and butter dotted the table, with Mama's prize chocolate pot standing sentinel near her seat. The faint spicy smell of chocolate tinged the room with warmth. There was nothing quite like Mama's chocolate on a chilly morning.

Papa appeared at the breakfast table—something he had not done since Mr. Collins had been staying with them. Though he hid behind his newspaper, it was pleasant to have his company again. Mama's nerves were still frail, and she took no pleasure in Lydia's recounting of the Lucas's party. She rallied briefly as Wickham's attentions to Elizabeth were described, but failed again at the news of Mary King's new fortune.

"An heiress?" Mama gasped and pulled out her handkerchief. She fanned her face and gasped for breath. "Ten thousand pounds?"

"Her grandfather left it to her. Who knew she was in line for such favor? I wish someone would die and leave me ten thousand pounds." Lydia crossed her arms and huffed.

"She got ever so much attention last night. It was quite shocking really. All the officers seemed to notice her for the first time. She is such a nasty freckled thing!" Kitty sniffed and buttered a slice of toast, crumbs flying to and fro.

"A fortune will always make a woman far more attractive than she deserves to be." Mama's face contorted into the horrid little mocking gesture she reserved to express her deepest disapproval. "Miss Mary King certainly does not compare to your beauty, Lydia dear, nor to Jane's."

However, to herself and Kitty … no that thought was not helpful at all. Best not pursue that line of thinking. Elizabeth spooned preserves on her toast.

"Not that any of your beauty seems to matter at all these days. I cannot at all understand the behavior of these young men."

"I cannot imagine it has changed very much from our own young days." Papa sipped his coffee.

"Has not changed? Has not changed? How can

you possibly say that? I see few similarities at best."
Mama dabbed her neck with her handkerchief.

"A pretty face has always attracted attention, but a
fortune, that motivates a man to act."

"What are you saying, sir? What do you mean of
your own daughters?" Mama slapped the table. Glasses shook and china rattled.

"Only that they should not be surprised that Miss
King is receiving so much attention now. It is normal,
and it will pass. She will marry soon enough, I am
sure, and the neighborhood shall return to normal. A
little patience will restore nearly all their beaux to
them."

"So, you believe Mr. Bingley will return to us as
well? I cannot understand his absence. It is entirely
irresponsible. He owes it to the neighborhood—"

"Madam, the only thing he owes is his rent to Mr.
Bascombe." Papa did not lift his eyes from his paper.

"Be that as it may, I cannot fathom why he should
continue to stay away."

Jane closed her eyes and turned her face aside.

Had not Mama already discussed this issue suffi-
ciently? Did she think there were new answers to be
found now?

"Perhaps Mr. Bingley was not as fond of Meryton
as we thought." Elizabeth avoided Mama's gaze as
she spoke. "It is very possible that his affections were
of the common and transient sort. Now he is in London, presumably among very pleasing society and
surroundings. I am sure he finds enough to delight
him that he has little memory of his time here among
us."

"Little memory! Little memory! How can you say
such a thing? How can you speak of your sister so?

She has been very ill-used indeed. You suggest that she is not the most beautiful creature of his acquaintance? How can you speak of her so?" Mama gesticulated wildly, nearly knocking over the chocolate pot.

"Please, Mama." Jane laid her hand on Elizabeth's wrist. "How can you imagine she would be so unkind?"

"You heard what she said as well as me. What else could she possibly mean?"

Papa caught Elizabeth's gaze and rolled his eyes. At least he did not believe Mama's accusations. He slid his chair back. "Only that Mr. Bingley is as many young men, bent on his own pleasure and rather oblivious to the opinions of those with little connection to him at all."

"Little connection? You saw how attached he was to our dear Jane. How can you call that little connection?"

Papa muttered and shook his head.

"It is well Mama, truly—" Jane's fingers tightened on Elizabeth's arm, the only real testament to her distress that she would reveal.

"No, it is not. It is not well at all. I declare I do not understand how you can say that." Mama shook her head and shoulders, as if that would repel the very idea. "I simply cannot accept that he was not very attached to our dear Jane. He might not return for the winter as has been said, but I am quite certain the summer will find him returned to us. I will hear no other opinion." Mama's snort dared them to disagree.

"Then I suppose there is little left to discuss." Papa rose, dipped his head, and left.

Mama turned to Elizabeth with a look that never boded well.

Elizabeth dabbed her lips with her napkin and rose. "Pray excuse me." She hurried away.

A walk in the garden might be nice. A walk anywhere would be a distinct improvement to another minute in Mama's company. Jane's forbearance might be equal to the task, but Elizabeth's.

Crisp, clear autumn air greeted her with sharpness in her nose and a chill across the back of her neck. She pulled her spencer a little closer. Papa stood near the bare-limbed wilderness as if contemplating whether or not to partake of its pleasures. She strode to his side and slipped her hand into the crook of his arm.

"Shall we walk?" She looked up at him, but he did not look back.

He grunted and matched her steps.

The soft moss that covered the path hushed their footfalls to gentle whispers, lost on the breeze that wafted the scents of autumn on its wings.

Papa's warmth beside her and the comforting scent of his soap and shaving oil spoke of safety and stability, all the things Mama thought ephemeral. Perhaps Mama was right, but for now, maybe just now, all was well. She leaned her head on his shoulder.

"So, Lizzy, your sister is crossed in love. I congratulate her. Next to being married, a girl likes to be crossed in love a little now and then. It is something to think of, and gives her a sort of distinction among her companions."

"I think it is a distinction she would be happy to do without."

"Perhaps you are correct, but still I think it should give your mother many hours of comfort and conversation during the coming winter." He clucked his tongue. "When we are all in want for something to distract us from the cold, she might remind us all of the ruined expectations caused by Mr. Bingley's infidelity."

"I think a game of chess would suit me better."

"And I too my dear." He patted her hand. "When is your turn to come? You will hardly bear to be long outdone by Jane."

"I do not take your meaning, sir."

"Being crossed in love, Lizzy. Let now be your time. There are officers enough at Meryton to disappoint all the young ladies in the country. Let Wickham be your man. He is a pleasant fellow, and would jilt you creditably." Papa's sense of humor was notably peculiar, but this was odd even for him.

"Thank you, but a less agreeable man would satisfy me. We must not all expect Jane's good fortune."

"True, but it is a comfort to think that, whatever of that kind may befall you, you have an affectionate mother who will always make the most of it."

She chuckled, more because he would expect it than because she felt the mirth of it. Whatever could he mean? She might be mistaken, but no, it sounded very much as though he were, in his own way, encouraging her toward Mr. Wickham.

He had never before remarked so on a young man, and there had been opportunity. Why would he do so now? Perhaps he was only teasing as he was apt to do, but perhaps not. Could he be as concerned as Mama for their future?

A chill breeze blew and cooled her flushed cheeks.

Perhaps Mama's nervous flutters were far less silly than she thought. How much danger were she and her sisters in? Were the hedgerows as near as Mama intimated?

Elizabeth faltered a step and struggled to keep up under the weight that descended upon her shoulders.

"There, there now, do not take it so hard. I hardly imagine it shall be much of an onus to you." He held his hand over hers and paused until she found her footing again.

He was right in that. Continuing to enjoy Mr. Wickham's company was hardly a burden … certainly not compared to bearing the responsibility of securing the family's future. It was not as though he asked her to marry Mr. Darcy.

December 23, 1811 Meryton

Monday morning, bright and clear, proved perfect for traveling and welcoming the Gardiners to spend Christmas at Longbourn. The children tumbled out of the Gardiners' coach into Jane's waiting arms. Though three hours was not really so very long to be confined to a carriage, their young cousins would be hard pressed to agree and were ready to follow Jane into the garden to spend pent up energy.

Jane adored the Gardiner children. They brought the first genuine smile to her face since Miss Bingley's letter had come. One more reason to appreciate the Gardiners' arrival.

Mama waited inside the parlor with tea and refreshments on the low table in front of her. Afternoon sun warmed the room invitingly, dust motes playing in the sunshine. In the warmth, the pale, floral-print curtains reminded Elizabeth of the garden in early summer.

"How lovely all this looks!" Aunt Gardiner placed her large basket on the sofa as she stood just behind. "You are so very good to have this waiting for us."

"Aunt Gardiner!" Lydia and Kitty burst in, the door hitting the wall behind, adding another small dark mark to the paint where the door handle struck.

Aunt Gardiner extended her hands and greeted them with kisses on their cheeks. "How well you both look! See what I have brought you from town!" She opened her basket and handed bundles to them all.

"Do sit down girls and act like the refined young ladies you are." Mama gestured them all toward seats around the table, but that did not stop Kitty and Lydia from dancing in the sunbeams.

"The ribbon I longed for! Oh look Mama!" Lydia draped a length of pink embroidered ribbon across her bodice. "Will it not look well on my sprigged muslin gown?"

"Indeed it will, child. You are so thoughtful, sister." Mama unwrapped a bundle of silk flowers. "You chose these to go with my blue gown."

"Indeed, I did. I am certain you will find some good use for them." Aunt Gardiner smiled broadly.

Kitty bounced on her toes. "Oh, oh, the lace is so beautiful! I cannot wait to put it on my bonnet!"

"I hope you will be able to do so before we leave. I would very much like to see your work."

"Thank you for the music," Mary's tone was demure, but her eyes glittered.

Somehow Aunt Gardiner always chose the most thoughtful gifts. The beaded reticule suited Jane as did the book Elizabeth had once borrowed from the circulating library on her last visit to London.

"Surely you must be peaked by now. Sit down and refresh yourself." Mama began serving tea and talking of all the changes in the neighborhood since the Gardiners' last visit.

Aunt Gardiner listened politely to Mama's list of grievances and complaints at how ill-used they had all been. Two of her girls had been on the point of marriage. Yet, still after all that, there was nothing in it.

Jane blushed and examined her new reticule closely. Elizabeth steeled her spine to keep from squirming in her seat.

"I do not blame Jane, for Jane would have got Mr. Bingley, if she could. But, Lizzy! It is very hard to think that she might have been Mr. Collins's wife by this time, had not it been for her own perverseness. He made her an offer in this very room, and she refused him."

"But sister—" Aunt Gardiner reached for her hand.

Mama pulled back. "The consequence of it is that Lady Lucas will have a daughter married before I have. Worse yet, Longbourn estate is just as much entailed as ever. The Lucases are very artful people indeed. They are all for what they can get. I am sorry to say it of them, but so it is."

"Mama!" Jane's eyes pleaded for reprieve.

"It makes me very nervous and poorly, to be thwarted so in my own family, and to have neighbors who think of themselves before anybody else. However, your coming just at this time is the greatest of comforts. I am very glad to hear what you have to tell us of long sleeves."

None of Mama's news was truly new to Aunt Gardiner, having heard it all in prior correspondence with Elizabeth. Perhaps because of that, or her general level of compassion for her nieces, she was only too pleased to turn the conversation to how long sleeves were being worn in town.

Half an hour later, Aunt Gardiner begged leave to stretch her legs outside. Elizabeth offered to show her the changes in the garden, and they hurried off together before Mama could protest.

The evening chill would set in soon. They had perhaps an hour before the cold—and waning light—would drive them in. But for now, they could enjoy the colors of the sunset as they painted the autumn blossoms and the dry leaves and grass that crunched underfoot.

"It seems likely to have been a desirable match for Jane," Aunt said. "I am sorry it went off. But these things happen so often! A young man, such as you describe Mr. Bingley, so easily falls in love with a pretty girl for a few weeks. When accident separates them, he so easily forgets her. These sorts of inconstancies are very frequent."

"An excellent consolation in its way, but it will not do for us. We do not suffer by accident. What think you of it when the interference of friends persuades a young man of independent fortune to think no more of a girl with whom he was violently in love only a few days before?" Elizabeth plucked a tall stalk of grass and swished it across her path.

"But that expression of 'violently in love' is as often applied to feelings which arise from an half-hour's acquaintance, as to a real, strong attachment. Pray, how violent was Mr. Bingley's love?"

"I never saw a more promising inclination. He was growing quite inattentive to other people, and wholly engrossed by her. Every time they met, it was more decided and remarkable. At his own ball he offended two or three young ladies by not asking them to dance. I spoke to him twice myself without receiving an answer. Could there be finer symptoms? Is not general incivility the very essence of love?"

"Oh, yes—of exactly that kind of 'love' which I suppose him to have felt. Poor Jane! I am sorry for her, because, with her disposition, she may not get over it immediately. It had better have happened to you, Lizzy; you would have laughed yourself out of it sooner. Do you think she would be prevailed on to go back to London with us? Change of scene might be of service." Aunt Gardiner raised a knowing eyebrow. "Perhaps a little relief from home may be as useful as anything."

"What an excellent scheme, I think she will be most pleased of it."

"And tell me of yourself, now. Are you sure you are unaffected by your brush with marriage?" Aunt Gardiner clasped Elizabeth's hands.

"I assure you, Mr. Collins has left me utterly unscathed. I shall not repine his attentions."

"I am relieved to hear it, for it seems your mother is intent on making you regret your choices."

Elizabeth shrugged "I have grown accustomed to it, I think. And she is not so very intent. She is now recommending that I encourage the attentions of yet another young man."

"Indeed, this is news to me. Pray tell me more of him."

"He is an officer in the militia and he hails from

Derbyshire. That alone should ensure your approval of him."

"My approval?" Aunt stopped short and stared into Elizabeth's face. "That you desire it suggests there is some attachment on your part."

"I assure you, neither of us is violently in love. He is a pleasant gentleman. You will see for yourself I am sure. Mama has many engagements planned for whilst you are here. I have no doubt there will be opportunity to see you are introduced."

"I shall look forward to it." Aunt's expression did not quite agree with the sentiment.

"So shall I. I would value your opinion on the gentleman both my parents seem to approve of."

December, 24 1811 Christmas Eve. London

The morning of Christmas Eve, Darcy sat in his study, sipping his coffee, a plate of still warm toast and jam pushed off to the side of his desk. Although the morning room was probably a mite more comfortable, it was also a reminder that he was alone in the house. Ordinarily, he relished his solitude, but this year was oddly different. There was something accusing in the way the empty chairs stared back at him.

The neatly ordered shelves and cabinets of the office offered solace and a reminder of his place and purpose in the world. Even without a family of his own, an entire estate depended on him—he had reason and purpose in what he did and that was satisfying—if a little lonely.

He reached for a small pile of letters atop a stack of papers that required his attention. Bingley's handwriting all but reached out and waved a friendly 'hello'. The man had a distinct hand—not at all neat or regular, but much like Bingley himself, friendly and outgoing. The seal was thin and sloppily pressed, breaking off quite easily. Bingley must have been in a hurry sending it. But he usually was in a hurry doing such things.

Stretched and loopy scrawl reminded Darcy of how much his presence was anticipated at the Bingley Christmas party. How thoughtful, if entirely unsubtle. But Bingley had seen him shun gatherings at the last minute often enough, it was hardly surprising that he exerted himself to avoid that outcome.

Darcy penned a brief, but positive response. He would indeed attend Bingley's gathering. Even if only for a short time, he would be there. He sealed the note and set it aside.

Two other letters of business could wait for a response. Beneath them, the housekeeper had left him several lists to review. The menu for the servants' Christmas feast? Why did he need to evaluate that? Oh—there would be no meal cooked for Darcy House that day, but it was still fitting that the servants should have something special. But what was appropriate? Were those not matters for the mistress of the house—who did not currently exist.

Darcy sighed a haggard breath and raked his hair. Was it wrong to hate the way household matters left him feeling incompetent? Best to trust the housekeeper's judgement on this matter. That is what she was employed for. He set the list aside and picked up another.

A list of the boxes to be prepared for Boxing Day and their contents—for the servants, the tradesmen and one for the foundling house. There were so many—not that the number was a problem. The Darcys had always been known for their generosity. But so many details to keep in mind. It was as if the housekeeper prepared the boxes not just for their recipients, but their entire families, too.

He was supposed to approve those as well? His mother would have known exactly what to provide. For that matter, it sounded just like the sort of thing Miss Elizabeth would be involved with at Longbourn. She was so attentive to the needs of those around her. What would she say to such lists? Would she appreciate their efficiency, or would she decry them as cold and hard, preferring spontaneity?

The brass knocker on the front door rapped, and it squealed open. Who would be calling at this hour?

Darcy closed his eyes to hear. A high-pitched boyish voice and the scent of evergreens wafted in on the breeze. That was the smell of Christmas at Pemberley.

They had always cut boughs to decorate the house on Christmas Eve. A great many of them were required to decorate such a large house. He and Father would take the donkey cart and fill it to overflowing with evergreens. When Mother had her fill of them, they would take the cart to the alms houses of the parish so they too might enjoy the scents and colors of the season. True, it was not strictly a need, but sometimes, Mother said, the heart needed charity as well.

"Are evergreens wanted here?" a boyish voice asked.

"Well, now, I do not know," the housekeeper replied.

Darcy briskly strode to the front door. "Yes, they are."

The housekeeper stepped aside, revealing a young boy, perhaps eight. With ginger hair, freckles, and a dirty face, he might have been a child living on the Pemberley estate.

"How many will you have, sir?" The boy gestured at a handcart heaped with boughs.

Darcy selected an armload, enough to adorn the morning room. "I will have these for the house." He handed them to the housekeeper. "But I will purchase the entire load."

"All of them?" The boy's eyes grew wide.

"Yes, all, but for that, you must do one additional thing."

"What, sir?" He all but bounced with anticipation.

"I want you to take these to the alms houses of the parish, and give them to the widows and children who live there. Do not fail, though, for I will ask the vicar to check up on your work."

"Of course, sir, of course. I will do just as you say!"

"Then here is an extra penny for your efforts." Darcy pressed a few coins into the boy's hand and watched until he disappeared around the corner.

How long had it been since he sent evergreens to the widows? Far too long. He returned to the study, pulled out a fresh sheet of foolscap, and dipped his pen. There would be some additional instructions for Christmastide at Darcy House.

Did Georgiana know of that tradition at Pemberley? She was of age that she should. Some girls her age were already running their own households. She should learn Pemberley's ways, both to carry on at

Pemberley and to take to the home she would manage someday, just as Pemberley's future mistress would bring her own traditions with her. What might those new traditions be?

Miss Elizabeth's face flashed in his mind. He closed his eyes and shook his head.

Best not let his mind wander—a letter to Georgiana was in order.

December 25, 1811 Christmas morning. Meryton

Christmas morning dawned cool and clear. The Gardiner children dashed down the stairs, the rest of the family close behind. Mama ushered them all into the crowded morning room festooned with evergreen boughs and holly. Small bundles wrapped in paper or pretty fabric lay at every place around the overflowing table.

"Jane, take your cousins to their seats. Kitty, help her. Sister, your place is there by the window, and brother opposite her." Mama pointed each to their seat.

She had not looked so happy since the whole affair with Mr. Collins began. Nothing made her so cheerful as to play generous hostess to family and friends.

Papa shuffled in and sat in his customary place. Good thing Mama had not tried to move him. "I believe we are all assembled as you requested, Mrs. Bennet."

"Indeed we are." Mama waved toward the door, and Hill and the maid entered bearing trays with tea, coffee and two pots of chocolate.

"Oh, oh, chocolate!" Aunt Gardiner's oldest daughter squealed. "May we all have some?"

"Indeed you may, all of you children, if you wish." Mama looked very pleased with herself.

Aunt Gardiner nodded at her children. They clapped and bounced in their chairs.

"Hill, you may serve the chocolate. Go on now, open your gifts." Mama waved at the children.

This was always Elizabeth's favorite part of the Gardiners' Christmas visit. Watching the children's faces as they unwrapped their treasures never grew tiresome. What could match a little boy's eyes lighting up over a box of tin soldiers or his sister's squeals of delight at miniature furniture for her baby house? Though Elizabeth appreciated the delicate lace fichu Mama selected for her, it was still nothing to the pleasure of seeing the children.

The children were disappointed to have to put their treasures away when it was time for the family to walk to the church. But Jane, with a little help from Kitty and Lydia, soon had them returned to their general good cheer.

After service, Papa and Uncle Gardiner took the children with them to the baker to pick up the Christmas goose. Mama led the ladies home, assigning tasks as they went. With the officers joining them for Christmas dinner, there was ever so much to be done to prepare. It did not seem to ease Mama's mind that the dining room and drawing room had been thoroughly readied for the event the day before.

Indeed, it was good that it had been done, since Papa did not see fit to hire more servants, they still had to inspect the plate and make sure it was thoroughly polished and that the table was properly set, the maid was, after all, often lax in her duties. And the greenery! The children had helped the day before, arranging it throughout the house, but, bless the little ones, they did not know how to place it properly and it all must be rearranged before guests arrived.

Aunt Gardiner glanced at Lizzy. She was such a patient woman, choosing not to take umbrage at Mama's nervous flutterings. Instead she offered to manage the placement of the holiday greenery herself so that Mama could attend to matters of the kitchen.

❧ Chapter 5

December 25, 1811 Christmas Evening. London

DARCY STEPPED DOWN from his carriage and stared at Bingley's front door. He tugged his shirt cuffs from beneath his jacket and straightened his cravat. The butler opened the imposing door.

Doffing his hat and great coat, he paused in the candlelit vestibule. Evergreen and holly boughs, tied with red ribbon, draped the sides of the doors, scenting the air with green—was green even a scent? It seemed as though it should be. Muffled conversation floated down from the drawing room. Fragrances wafted from the kitchen, boar's head and was it ... yes, mince pie.

At Pemberley, mince pie was never served until after the Christmas feast. So much food was prepared for family and guests, tenants and servants, the cooling tables bowed with abundance. No less than three were erected in the morning room to manage the overflow from the kitchen. After the feast, baskets were sent around to tenants and the parish poor, and still there was more left over.

Mrs. Reynolds and Cook would gather all that remained. Every free hand in the house would be marshalled to chop and mix filling and pastry crust for piles and piles of mince pies. For at least a fortnight afterwards, no one came within a quarter mile of Pemberley without having a mince pie pushed into their hands.

His mouth watered, and he licked his lips.

"Mr. Darcy!" Miss Bingley called from halfway up the marble stairs. She wore a pink-purple gown, some color that was supposed to be very fashionable and expensive and probably was, considering the many yards of silk and froth that draped her tall form. Her ostrich feather, dyed to match, bobbed in time with her steps. "I am so glad you have joined us."

"Thank you for your gracious invitation." He bowed.

For all her faults, Miss Bingley was an excellent hostess. She had, after all, managed a remarkable feat, pulling together the Netherfield ball in but a fortnight. In all likelihood, she had been planning this event the entire month they had been in London.

"Will you join us in the drawing room? We are waiting on just a few more guests to join us before we dine." She led him upstairs.

The dull roar of many people grew loud enough to be felt as much as heard. Evergreen and holly bedecked the stair rail and wax candles brightened every corner of the hall with fragrance and flickering light. The drawing room, aided by many mirrors, seemed even brighter. Vases, filled with tasteful arrangements of laurel and Christmas roses, pulled the eye around the room to admire the fine furnishings and accessories acquired on Bingley's grand tour.

His taste ran slightly to the side of garish; Miss Bingley influenced him toward that. But he could also use a pointer or three in the art of restraint.

"May I introduce you to our other guests?" She gestured around the drawing room.

Darcy glanced about the crowded room. People, some familiar, many not, filled every available space. A group clustered around the fainting sofa, hiding its outlandish floral print—that was a blessing. Others gathered in the far more tolerable grouping of ladder-back chairs near the pianoforte. He clenched his fists so as not to tug at his collar. How did one not suffocate in the presence of so many?

Thank Providence! None of those horrid contributors to the society columns were lurking in the crowd. What more could he honestly ask of an evening?

Still, he hesitated. Acquaintances were a tricky thing. He would be expected to remember and acknowledge these new connections when next they met, something he was ill-equipped to do. Names and faces blurred and fogged in his mind, forever leading him into awkward social blunders.

But what greater offense would he cause by refusing her simple request?

"Darcy!" Bingley appeared out of the throng. "Simply capital to see you tonight. Come, I must have you meet Sir Andrew and Miss Aldercott. He is the most delightful fellow." He beckoned Darcy to follow him to the opposite side of the room, describing the pair in question as they went.

Sir Andrew had a penchant for fine horses, but was troubled by gout in his left leg, so he rarely rode any more. Horse racing had become his passion, but he tended to bet too much.

Miss Aldercott was his daughter and possessed a substantial fortune. She was usually found in the company of her two pugs, who, it was said, looked rather like her brother and sister—she was the beauty of the family. She was an excellent horsewoman, but preferred to drive than ride. Her little phaeton had recently been repainted, and she was hoping to learn to drive her father's curricle soon. By the time they actually found Sir Andrew and Miss Aldercott, it was as if he had the pleasure of their acquaintance for years.

That was the difference when Bingley introduced someone new. His endless ramble offered enough to remember those new acquaintances tolerably well and have some idea upon what to conduct a conversation. Did Bingley know he was so useful or was it merely a happy coincidence?

If the latter, Bingley enjoyed more good luck in a fortnight than any man was entitled to in a lifetime. If the former, he was a good deal more clever than any gave him credit for. In either case, he was a very good friend.

Sir Andrew and Miss Aldercott proved interesting acquaintances indeed. Father and daughter both had distinct opinions on the likelihood of purchasing a matched team of four and the proper price to pay for such. Darcy agreed more with the father than the daughter. Even so it was a memorable conversation to have had with a young woman. Almost as memorable as some of the conversations he had enjoyed at Netherfield, with Miss Elizabeth.

Miss Bingley pushed her way through the milling guests and whispered something in Bingley's ear.

"Capital!" He cleared his throat and raised his voice "I have just been informed, dinner is served."

"Ladies," Miss Bingley led them to the doorway.

The ladies sorted themselves by rank and proceeded to the dining room in what unfortunately resembled a parade of bobbing peahens.

Was it Bingley's influence that dissuaded Miss Bingley from insisting upon the modern convention of having the gentlemen escort the ladies in? Or did she just prefer more traditional sensibilities? Whichever it was, he was grateful to avoid another potentially awkward situation.

Bingley elbowed him on the way into the dining room. "You ought to know Caroline expects you to sit beside her at dinner."

"Have you no knight or baronet or grey-haired gentleman to take that place? Sir Andrew should surely have that honor."

"Sir Andrew is looking for a wife and would prefer to sit beside the widow Garnet." Bingley chuckled and faded off to address another guest.

Meryton

Later that night, Elizabeth paced the very clean drawing room, waiting for their guests to arrive. Every surface was dusted and polished to reflect the light from an extra measure of candles. Fresh evergreen and holly filled the room with the season's fragrances, tied with cheery red bows. It should have been a very pleasing scene, but the tension in the room threatened to smother her.

"Why do you not take a seat, Lizzy?" Aunt Gardiner patted the seat beside her.

"I should surely run mad if I do." Elizabeth offered an apologetic smile.

"It seems like they are so long in arriving tonight. I cannot wait for the officers to get here." Lydia peered out the window, wrapping the gold wool curtain around her shoulders and tangling the fringe in her fingers.

"They are such agreeable company, so gallant and always in search of a spot of fun." Kitty fidgeted in her seat.

"Do sit still. It is unbecoming to twitch about like a hound waiting to be fed." Mary folded her hands in her lap and adjusted her posture to something entirely stiff and proper. "And unwind yourself from the curtains before you tear them off the wall entirely."

"You need not be so disagreeable. It is not as if you are anticipating the arrival of anyone special." Lydia sniffed and made an ugly face.

"Lydia!" Aunt Gardiner slapped the sofa cushion.

"Well, it is true. None of the officers like her for she is so very dull."

Mary's cheeks colored. Her lips pressed tight into something not quite a frown, but certainly nothing less.

"Your opinions are not helpful, nor are they kind."

"But they are true," Lydia whispered.

"Lydia!" Jane's eyes bulged the way they usually did when someone said something distasteful.

Lydia snorted and tossed her head.

The front door creaked and voices drifted upstairs.

"Oh, oh, someone is here! I think I recognize Sanderson's voice." Kitty clapped softly.

Lydia and Kitty pinched their cheeks and checked their bodices. Mary moved to the pianoforte.

"Would you favor us with a light welcoming piece?" Aunt Gardiner asked, but it was more a direction than a question.

At least Mary did not seem too disgruntled by it. If anything, she looked pleased to have her accomplishments recognized. Perhaps she would have some pleasure this evening after all.

Mama swept in with several officers in her wake.

"Sister, may I introduce Lieutenants Wickham, Denny and Sanderson."

Aunt Gardiner rose and curtsied. "Pleased to make your acquaintance, I am sure."

"Thank you for admitting us to your acquaintance, madam." Wickham bowed, his eyes shining.

He always seemed to know the right thing to say.

Lydia and Kitty drew Denny and Sanderson away as Hill ushered Aunt and Uncle Philips in. Jane excused herself to attend them.

Aunt Gardiner cocked her head and lifted her eyebrow at Elizabeth. "My niece tells me you are from Derbyshire, sir."

"Indeed, I am madam. Are you familiar with the county?" He stepped a little closer.

"I spent my girlhood there, in the area of Lambton."

Wickham's eyes brightened, and his face softened with a smile so compelling even a French officer would have been drawn in. "I lived on an estate very near there, Pemberley if you know it."

"I do indeed. One of the loveliest places I have ever seen. We were by no means in such a way to keep company with that family, but we heard much of their good name whilst we lived there." Aunt Gardiner's eyes always shone when she spoke of her girlhood home.

"I was privileged to live on the Pemberley estate, my father was steward there."

"Then you were well-favored indeed. Have you been there recently?"

"Very little since the death of old Mr. Darcy. While old Darcy was a very good and kind man, and very well disposed toward myself, I am afraid his son did not inherit his father's noble traits." He glanced at Elizabeth, such suffering in his eyes, her own misted.

She nodded for him to continue. Surely Aunt Gardiner must be interested to hear his account in all its fullness.

"I have no desire to burden you with such tales as would dampen your spirits on this very fine occasion. Let us talk of acquaintances we may share in common. Did you know the old apothecary there, Mr. Burris I believe his name."

"He was a great favorite of my father's."

"Of mine as well." Though Wickham had been there little in the past five years, it was yet in his power to give her fresher intelligence of her former friends than she had been in the way of procuring.

It did not take too long for their recollection of shared society to turn to a discussion of old Mr. Darcy's character, whom both liberally praised. The conversation then naturally moved on to the current Mr. Darcy and his treatment of Wickham.

"I grant you, that I recall the younger Mr. Darcy spoken of as a very proud, ill-natured boy, but the charges you lay at his feet are quite alarming. I am surprised you have not been able to bring some kind of influence to bear against him." Something in Aunt's expression suggested she was weighing his words carefully, the way she did when her sons brought her an intriguing tale.

"Would that were possible, madam, I would probably be the better for it. In truth, though, I still hold his father in far too high a regard to be able to take action against his son. The thought of bringing old Mr. Darcy pain is far too disturbing to brook."

"But surely you must consider how his own son's behavior would distress him. He might have been very pleased to see its improvement. I know that to be the case if it were one of my own children charged with such heartlessness." Aunt chewed her lower lip.

"You might be very right, but surely you can see I am not the one suited by station or inclination to bring correction to such a man. So, I shall continue on as I have been, grateful to such friends as I still have around me. I am truly blessed to have some very staunch supporters."

"I imagine so." Aunt's eyebrows raised into an elegant arch. "You demonstrate very great forbearance, quite the model of gentlemanly behavior."

There was something the faintest bit sharp in Aunt's tone. Elizabeth tried to catch her eye, but she looked over Elizabeth's shoulder.

Elizabeth glanced back. Jane and Aunt Philips approached.

"How are your enjoying your visit, sister? Is not the company tonight delightful?" Aunt Philips extended her hands toward Aunt Gardiner, but glowered at Elizabeth.

Aunt Gardiner took Aunt Philips's hands and kissed her cheeks. "Indeed it is. But we always appreciate the hospitality at Longbourn. I should hardly expect anything else."

"Mr. Wickham, it is especially nice to see you and the other officers here tonight. We have missed your company of late."

"I regret any discomfiture I might have caused, but I am honored my absence might have been noticed." Wickham bowed from his shoulders.

"Of course, it was, of course it was. I am very pleased to see you, Miss Lizzy, are not above keeping such very plain company with us tonight." Aunt Phillips's lip curled just the way Mama's did when she was angry.

Elizabeth had been seeing a great deal of that expression lately.

"Whatever do you mean?" Aunt Gardiner's honey-eyed tone had been known to placate tired children and churlish adults alike. "Elizabeth is always a sparkling companion."

"In company she deigns to keep, of course she is. It is just possible her opinion of herself has grown a mite higher than it should." Aunt Phillips's eyes narrowed far too much like Mama's.

Elizabeth's face grew cold, but her cheeks burned.

Mama burst into the room. "Shall we all to dinner?"

"Might I escort you, Miss Elizabeth?" Mr. Wickham offered his arm.

Elizabeth muttered something, curtsied to her aunts and took Mr. Wickham's arm. He led her through the crowded hall toward the dining room.

"Thank you." The words barely slipped past her tight throat. "Pray, excuse my Aunt's indelicate choice of conversation."

"What indelicate choice? You do not think her conversation reflected in any way upon you, do you? I have found when people resort to dialogue which some may consider disagreeable it is most often at-tributable to indigestion."

Elizabeth snickered under her breath.

"Perhaps it would be wise to suggest Mrs. Philips have a few words with her cook. A change in diet might be the very thing to relieve her discomfort and improve her general disposition. See there how her husband is red in the face and his hand is pressed so obviously to his belly? I would venture to say he too may be suffering from indigestion. It is his cook and no one else to blame."

It would seem Mr. Wickham did not or chose not to see Mama at Uncle Philips's side, speaking with great animation and casting sidelong glances toward Elizabeth.

"I shall suggest that to her." The words came eas-ier now. She forced her lips up into something resembling a smile.

"Ah, that is a far better expression for you, Miss Elizabeth. Unhappiness does not suit you at all."

"It appears it is difficult to be unhappy in your presence sir. Do you make it your business to drive away such specters wherever they might appear?"

"I certainly do, what better occupation in life than to bring happiness wherever I wander?"

How very true, and how very different to Mr. Darcy. To maintain such a disposition despite the very great unfairness and trials he had faced. Mr. Wickham was truly too kind.

London

Inside the dining room, Darcy took his suggested seat. The room glittered with candles and crystal and mirrors, nearly as bright as day. Holly, laurel and evergreen draped every available surface. Their fresh aromas blended with those from the heavily laden table. Apparently the Bingleys employed an excellent Cook.

His mother had held such Christmas dinners at Pemberley. Truth be told, he missed them.

"I hope you see some choice here that pleases you, Mr. Darcy. Charles let slip a few of your favorites. I made certain they would be near your seat." Miss Bingley gestured toward the veal collops and roast cauliflower.

"Ah … yes … thank you. It was very gracious of you to go to such lengths for me. May I serve you from those dishes?"

"Thank you." She looked far too pleased at the suggestion.

He placed dainty portions on her plate. If she were anything like his Mother, she would have eaten before her guests arrived so that she might focus on her role as hostess.

Once he had served himself and the neighboring ladies, the difficult part of the evening began. He needed to say something, but what?

That was one thing to be said of Elizabeth Bennet, she never forced on him the burden of starting a conversation. No, she took it upon herself to begin and offered such intriguing insights; it was easy to come in with his own. Never stilted or awkward, dialogue flowed so easily with her to facilitate. Her voice was a joy to listen to.

… and given the expectant look Miss Bingley wore, he still needed to say something.

"Have you enjoyed your move back to London?" Not the most original topic on his part, but it would do.

"I cannot tell you how much." Miss Bingley took a tiny sip of wine. "I am not well formed for life in such limited society as Meryton. The four and twenty families dined with by the Bennets did not suit my needs for companionship."

"I can imagine why."

A few of them might have appreciated Miss Bingley's fine manners. Though all who attended had lauded the Netherfield ball, still, as to establishing a genuine relationship, they had little in common.

She leaned in a little closer and dropped her voice a mite. "I have been remiss in offering you my thanks. Your help was pivotal in convincing Charles of the expedience of leaving that place. It is best for all of us that he should be away from the machinations of that … that Mrs. Bennet."

How could a woman like that have raised such a daughter as Elizabeth?

Miss Jane Bennet was a decent enough female, proper and demure, but not one easily moved to affection. Charles would suffer with an unattached woman. That alone was reason enough to separate them. But Elizabeth, witty, vivacious and passionate—the family was almost worth tolerating for the privilege of her society.

"Bingley does appear sanguine here." Darcy glanced down the table toward Bingley, chatting with his neighbor.

"I am not so certain. He has been quite the brown study over the last fortnight. But it is for his own good. We all bear it as well as we can."

"A brown study? That is difficult to imagine of him. He seems cheerful tonight."

"He has a great company around him now, and that always cheers him. I have events planned every day until Twelfth Night in the hopes of keeping him encouraged."

Was she correct? Bingley melancholy? Could he truly be so affected?

"I do wish only the best for my dear brother. But, I still worry about the success of our plans." She fluttered her eyelashes and pressed her fingertips to her chest.

"What cause have you for concern now you are away from Meryton?"

"Perhaps I am simply looking for vexation where none exists. I cannot help but remember the mention of an uncle in trade. Gardiner—I believe his name was—who lives in Cheapside. It seems that a determined mother might see her daughter to relatives in London with the hopes of finding a lost suitor."

"Do you really think she might do such a thing?" Darcy sat up straighter. More important, might she bring a sister—the right sister with her?

"In truth, I do not know. Perhaps I am being overly concerned." She shrugged, affecting a look of helplessness that was far from the truth.

"Would you like me to make discreet inquiries after this Mr. Gardiner? I cannot be certain of discovering anything—"

"I would be ever so grateful for your assistance. I do not wish to see Charles at risk again."

"Of course. I shall see what I might discover." For Bingley's sake, and his own.

Was it possible? Miss Elizabeth might come to London? Might she be away from her dreadful family even now?

His heart beat a little quicker. But what were the chances of this Gardiner fellow being any less dreadful than the rest of her relations? Even if he were not, they certainly did not mix in the same circles. Would he ever have the opportunity to see her?

Blast it all! The whole point of going to London was to avoid society with the Bennets.

"Are you well sir?"

Zounds, Miss Bingley was staring at him. Had his face turned some unusual color, or broken out in spots?

"Mr. Darcy?"

"Forgive me. I was just—just considering what you had said." His cheeks burned. If only she knew what he was thinking!

"I am so glad to know we are of one mind, sir. It is uncanny, is it not, how much alike we are, you and I." A coy, predatory look hung about her eyes, the look of a hunting bird circling its prey, lazily waiting for a convenient moment to strike.

He edged back. How had he missed it before? He knew the look well, but had thought himself safe enough amongst friends.

Miss Bingley called for the second course. The staff cleared away the dishes and revealed a fresh table cloth. More of his favorite dishes appeared at the head of the table.

At least now, Miss Bingley would turn the tables and converse with the lady on her left for the remainder of the meal. The knight beside Darcy already seemed to be in his cups. Annoying as it was, it meant Darcy had little to do but nod and offer sounds of affirmation as the knight prattled on. With his mind reeling, that was the best he could offer, so he ought to be thankful.

Bad enough one corner of his mind actively sought to forget one Elizabeth Bennet, whilst another conspired to find ways to seek her out should she chance to be in town. Now, he must also discourage Miss Bingley's matrimonial machinations without disenfranchising Bingley, too? He pressed his temples against a burgeoning headache. Truly, could this become more unpleasant?

Servants began putting out candles and a hush settled over the room. In the dim light of the remaining candles, a bright blue flame flared near the doorway. The housekeeper paraded the flaming cannonball shaped Christmas pudding in and placed it at the center of the table.

Mother always took pride in her Christmas puddings. She made Stir-it-up Sundays a grand affair, bringing in all the Matlock cousins she could gather. Spices and sweet fruit hung heavy in the hot, moist air of the kitchen as the cousins added ingredients and took their turn stirring. The last to go in were the family charms, silver and worn smooth with time; who would find their fortune with them added an air of mystery and anticipation to the event.

"…mind the charms in the pudding. Whoever finds one must call out their fortune." Miss Bingley sat down.

When had a slab of pudding appeared on his plate?

He took a small bite. Sweet, rich, spicy and soaked in brandy, exactly what a Christmas pudding should be. But it did not taste like Pemberley's.

Like home. Mrs. Reynolds would have to teach Elizabeth how to make Pemberley's someday.

He choked, coughing and sputtering on his bite of pudding. What was he thinking?

"Are you well, Mr. Darcy?" Miss Bingley asked wide-eyed.

He blotted his mouth with his napkin. "Forgive me, I am fine."

"You did not swallow a charm, did you?"

"No, just a crumb caught in my throat."

Across the table Bingley yelped—he had found the ring. Superstition promised him marriage in the next twelve-month. Another diner cried out she found the coin. Others followed in rapid succession.

His own pudding remained steadfastly void of any portent of his future, save the abundant raisins and brandy. Was that to be his lot in life, alone but for a drink in his hand and food on his table?

Meryton

For all Mama's fussing and fluttering, she did set one of the finest tables in the county. Candlelight sparkled off mirrors and crystal, filling every corner of the dining room with glistening warmth. The table and sideboards groaned under the weight of the dishes heaped with fragrant offerings. A huge goose lay near Papa's place, waiting for him to carve it. Elizabeth's mouth watered. Nothing tasted like a Christmas goose, its skin brown and crispy, the meat juicy and succulent.

Wickham held the chair for her and sat beside her, politely ignoring Lydia's cross look. What did she have to be cross about though? With Denny on one side and Sanderson on the other, it was not as if she would be in want of company and conversation herself.

Mama sat up very straight and rang a little silver bell. The door swung open and Hill appeared, holding a platter of roasted boar's head high. Her arms quivered under the massive offering.

Denny and Sanderson jumped to their feet, nearly knocking their chairs to the floor, and rushed to her aid. Together they made a lovely show of bringing the final dish to the table. Though Mama glared at Hill, she seemed very pleased at the officers' efforts and settled into her comfortable role, presiding over the table.

Wickham leaned toward her. "It has been quite some time since I have enjoyed such a Christmas feast."

"I hope you take every opportunity to enjoy this one."

He served her from the platter of roast potatoes nearby. "I will certainly do just that and lock it into my memory to treasure against times which may be far less agreeable."

"I am sure it is difficult to spend Christmastide away from one's home and family. The militia requires a great deal from you."

"I find that it gives back as much as it demands. It is not at all disagreeable for one in my state. The hardships do not at all compare to those I suffered the first Christmastide of my banishment from Pemberley."

"Banishment?"

"Perhaps that is too strong a word, you are right. It does not serve to be so melodramatic." He bowed his head. "You must forgive me, for it is the subject of some trying remembrances. Christmastide at Pemberley was a most wondrous season, filled with warmth and generosity. My family was invited to dine at Christmas dinner. A complete roast boar would be carried in by two footmen, goose, venison, and roast beef besides. I am sure it was a month's worth of food, for my little family at least, all brought to the table at once." He closed his eyes and licked his lips.

"I can imagine one might miss such extravagance."

"Pray, do not think I intended to belittle the wonderful hospitality Longbourn offers. Not at all. It has reminded me of much happier days. I am most grateful for the reminder."

Mama's silver bell rang. Hill and the maid hurried in to clear the first course. Platters and used dishes disappeared along with the table cloth. The second course dishes filled the empty table and fresh china appeared before them. Amidst the staff's efforts,

Aunt Gardiner caught her eye, tipped her head toward Wickham and raised her eyebrows.

Elizabeth allowed a hint of a smile and shrugged. He was very pleasant company. What did she expect?

Mama announced the dishes, but the platter of minced pies needed no introduction.

Wickham placed a small pie on her plate, along with black butter and spiced apples. The first minced pie of Christmastide was always agreeable, but somehow it would be nothing to the ones that would later be made from the leavings of the Christmas feast.

Mama's bell rang again, and she slipped out of the dining room. Hill circled the room, snuffing candles until only one in each corner remained.

Although Mama repeated this ritual every year, somehow the flaming pudding entering on the silver platter, held high in Mama's arms never lost its thrill. Blue brandy flames, glinting and multiplying in the mirrors and crystal, cast dancing shadows along the wall turning the dining room, for those brief moments, into a magical fairyland.

Too soon, the flames died down. The maid scurried about relighting candles, and the normal world reappeared with Mama standing over a great cannonball of plum pudding. She broke into it and served generous slices.

"Mind the charms!" Mama's smile seemed forced as she openly avoided looking at Elizabeth.

What better way to remind Mama of Elizabeth's transgressions than the pudding stirred up whilst she still had hopes of Mr. Collins? Pray let her not discover the ring, or better still, any charm in her pudding. Further notice from Mama could not be a good thing.

Elizabeth held her breath as the company partook of the pudding. Heavy, sweet, spicy and saturated with brandy, this was the taste of Christmas and family.

Uncle Gardiner laughed heartily. "What ho, what shall I do with this?" He held aloft a tiny thimble.

"Consider it for thrift, my dear." Aunt Gardiner winked at him.

Thank Providence that Mary was spared that omen!

Lydia squealed. "I have the coin! I shall come into a fortune."

Papa muttered something, but Elizabeth could not make it out. Probably best that way.

Wickham neatly pulled his slice apart with knife and fork. He dug in with his knife and lifted it to reveal a shining ring hanging on the blade.

"Now you've done it, Wickham!" Sanderson pointed at him, laughing.

"I would not go about showing that off, if I were you." Denny leaned back and held up open hands. "But whatever you do, keep it well away from me."

"So you shall be married this year, Mr. Wickham." Mama looked far too pleased.

Had there been any way to have achieved that end intentionally, Elizabeth would have thought Mama manufactured this result. But such a thing was not possible. Still, the smug way she settled into her seat and dug into her own pudding begged the question.

"You may threaten all you like." Wickham slid the ring off the knife and held it up in the candlelight. "But I have no fear of this innocent little ring."

Did he just wink? At her?

Heat crept over the crest of her cheeks, but Aunt Gardiner's brows drew a little lower over her eyes and her forehead creased.

London

Miss Bingley adjourned with the women to the drawing room, leaving Mr. Bingley to supply port and cigars to the men. Darcy welcomed the respite from the demands of conversation. Far less subtlety reigned here, permitting him to follow the conversations—on topics he understood and cared about—with greater ease and confidence.

In this company he could simply listen and not be judged uncivil. If he spoke, he could limit himself to subjects that interested him, ones he might speak on with authority. It was the one part of the evening that ended too soon.

Rejoining the ladies renewed those itchy woolen blanket feelings he had so recently discarded. He tried to excuse himself to Bingley and flee for the quiet of his own home, but Bingley would have none of it.

"I know we are nothing to Pemberley here, but—" Bingley's voice broke, and he looked away.

Was this the melancholy that Miss Bingley had noticed?

"Holidays spent in town are nothing to those in the country. They never are. We must make merry with what we have then, no?" He clapped Darcy's shoulder. "Allow me to make an introduction that I am sure will improve your evening in great measure."

"No, there is no need." Darcy inched back, but Bingley's hand between his shoulders propelled him into the crowded drawing room brimming with women. Bingley continued to nudge and prod him until they reached a group of three ladies sitting near the window.

"Lady Elizabeth Wesson, might I introduce you to my friend Mr. Fitzwilliam Darcy?"

The lady rose and curtsied.

This Elizabeth was the height of Miss Elizabeth Bennet, and, at least to an objective observer, far more beautiful. She sported classic features and a generous bosom that had occupied the attention of most of the men at dinner at one point or another.

"I am pleased to make your acquaintance, sir." She smiled just enough to be pleasant and proper. Nothing like the genuine, spontaneous smiles of Meryton's Elizabeth.

At least he knew how to manage such smiles. He bowed smartly. "Pleased to make your acquaintance."

Miss Bingley appeared at Bingley's elbow. "Lady Elizabeth, would you consider favoring us on the pianoforte?"

"Capital notion, Caroline. And Darcy, you can turn pages for her, even sing a few bars yourself."

Darcy's brow tightened into a hard knot. "I do not perform to strangers."

Bingley withered, as he deserved to for making such a suggestion.

"No offense to you, Lady Elizabeth. I will turn pages for you should you desire the service."

The lady's eyebrow arched and the corner of her lips lifted. Was she amused, puzzled or tolerant?

Reading ladies was far too complex.

"I believe I can reconcile myself to singing alone." Her voice was modulated, and musical, exactly as a lady's should be.

He followed her to the pianoforte. The whispers following in their wake were no surprise. He could hardly offer the time of day to a female before the rumors began. That was simply a part of the landscape now. He glanced over his shoulder. No, still no gossip writers, at least none that he recognized.

Lady Elizabeth sat at the pianoforte and placed a complicated score before her. Few would attempt to exhibit with such challenging music. Even Miss Bingley might think twice about making this the showcase of her skill. But Lady Elizabeth seemed made of sterner stuff. She calmly placed her hands on the keyboard and delighted the room with her mastery. Her hands flowed with effortless grace, so mesmerizing he nearly forgot to turn the pages. Her next piece was an old ballad, one of Darcy's favorites, sung and played just as flawlessly as the first.

Elizabeth Bennet would never have attempted the first piece, but she might have the second. She would not have been able to manage some of the fingerings and the highest notes were out of her range. No question, her performance would pale beside Lady Elizabeth's, and yet it would have had a compelling charm all its own. Perhaps even more appealing than the superior performance displayed before him.

Darcy escorted Lady Elizabeth away from the pianoforte. Every unattached man in the room, and some attached, watched her as they walked. Her grace and her figure made it difficult to look away. He should be pleased to have such a woman on his arm. Any man would.

"Would you care for a hand of cards, Mr. Darcy?" she asked, not looking directly at him.

He hated cards. A damn foolish way to lose money.

Miss Elizabeth did not play cards, at least not whilst she was at Netherfield. There she kept to her books, though at the same time she claimed to like many things, even cards.

What would it be like to play a hand with her? Her eyes would sparkle over her cards, never revealing the luck of her hand. She would banter and tease with each bet, taunting him to reveal more than he wanted, trying to sketch his character.

As she had in the ballroom at Netherfield. What conclusions had she drawn there? Surely she must be aware of his regard.

"Mr. Darcy?" Lady Elizabeth blinked up at him, eyes sparkling, lips smiling.

But her face was all wrong. She was the wrong Elizabeth. As pleasant and ladylike as she might be, she was the wrong Elizabeth. Any further time in her presence would surely drive him mad.

"Thank you, no. I must … excuse me …"

He bowed and strode off. Where was Bingley? He must be somewhere in the room.

There! Laughing and joking in a knot of young ladies hanging off his every word.

Too many long, purposeful strides brought him to Bingley, and he pulled Bingley aside.

"Darcy are you ill? You look like the very devil himself."

"I must take my leave. Pray give my regards to your sister."

"If you are unwell, you may certainly spend the night here with us. I shall have a room made up."

"No ... I ... I need to be ... home."

Bingley studied him. He glanced at Lady Elizabeth, brows rising, and nodded slowly. "I understand. I will call for your carriage."

"Thank you, I shall wait outside."

The cold night air embraced him, soothing the raw oppression of too much company burning his skin. Too much company and too little of the right Elizabeth.

He would conquer this. He must.

❧Chapter 6

December 26, 1811 Boxing Day. London

AFTER BINGLEY'S PARTY, sleep did not come easily. It rarely did after so large a social gathering, especially with the wrong Elizabeth haunting his dreams. By the time Darcy was dressed and in the soothing order and solitude of his study the next morning, the housekeeper was receiving the trades-men and handing out parcels for Boxing Day.

The maid came in with a breakfast tray which included the newspaper. Darcy poured himself a fragrant cup of coffee and settled into his favorite chair with his paper. He scanned for something of interest.

Theater announcements noted the opening of a new panto, Harlequin and Cinderella. Mother would have enjoyed that one—the panto was one of her favorite events. She probably would have insisted Father acquire tickets for the day after Boxing Day.

"But why not on Boxing Day?" he had asked.

"If for no other reason than to help you develop patience, Fitzwilliam." She kissed the top of his head and straightened the ruffled collar of his skeleton suit.

"I do not like patience, Mama."

"That is all right dear, none of us do. But it is an important virtue, nonetheless. In any case, we have important things to do on Boxing Day and will not have time for the theater until afterwards."

"What must we do?"

"Well, in the morning, the tradesmen will come for their boxes. Then, in the afternoon, we have invited the tenants to the manor for refreshments and games for the children. They shall have their boxes then as well. Then the alms houses of the parish must be visited and those boxes delivered."

"Why do we do all the bringing of boxes? Does no one bring us a box? That does not seem very fair."

"Life is not always fair, son. It is our privilege to be able to give in this season rather than receive. We have received so much already, it only seems right."

He had not understood his mother then, but she had been right. Rarely had he ever truly wanted for anything.

He sipped his coffee—just a touch too hot and too bitter—and smacked his lips. Perhaps that was what made this dilemma of Miss Elizabeth Bennet so difficult.

No point in dwelling upon it further. He pushed up from his chair.

Mother would have instructed him to go and greet some of the tradesmen as they visited. Company held little appeal, but at least this would adhere to a script he understood. That was far less disagreeable than the usual variety of socializing.

He walked back to the kitchen where the housekeeper chatted with two tradesmen enjoying small beer and a platter of bread, cold meat and cheese at a small worktable. Compared to Pemberley's kitchen, this one seemed small. But it was tidy, efficient and snug, filled with the homey fragrances of cooking food.

"Mr. Darcy." She curtsied and the two men, clean, but definitely worn around the edges, rose and bowed.

"Thank you very kindly for the box, sir," the older of the two men dipped his head again. "The missus has been doing poorly. The victuals and the shawl will go a long way in lifting her spirits."

"Indeed, sir," the other man clasped his hands behind his back and rocked on his heels. "Many thanks. Darcy House is known for its generosity. It be a privilege to be able to say that the cheese at your table comes from my establishment."

No doubt that same intelligence also improved his sales. Still, there was no harm in it either. Good work and good merchandise deserved reward.

Darcy forced himself to make the appropriate small talk and remain in the kitchen a full hour whilst several other tradesmen came and went. He would have to leave the housekeeper a few pounds extra when he left for Derbyshire. She, too, should be rewarded. Putting all those boxes together according to the needs of the families was no small task.

Mother had taken such care with the chore, it was the privilege of the estate's mistress to do so, she had said. Did Miss Elizabeth enjoy the undertaking at Longbourn …

No, no, no, that was not a helpful thought at all.

On his way to the study, the maid informed him Bingley had arrived and was waiting in the parlor.

"Good day, Bingley." Darcy gestured for him to sit down—it seemed the man had been pacing along the fireplace, leaving barely perceptible tracks on the dark patterned carpet before it.

When he was at the townhouse by himself, Darcy rarely used this room. Not so formal as the drawing room, the odd assortment of trinkets that line three curio cabinets and two sets of iron shelves brought back from various trips, invited too many thoughts of people he missed too dearly.

"You are looking much better than when you left last night. I am much relieved." Bingley settled back into a generous burgundy bergère and crossed one leg over the other.

"Yes, well, as you see, there is no reason for concern." Darcy sat on the dark grey and mahogany settee across from him.

"Are you certain? You did not look at all well—" Bingley peered at him.

"I am entirely well. Is that all you came for?"

Bingley laughed. "You know that is not the case. Have you forgotten how Caroline is the day after a major social event? She is doubly so when it is an event she has hosted. You would think all the worrying was done and over with the event, but no. She is ever concocting reasons for fear and trepidation: what will people be saying, what might appear in the society pages, would there be invitations extended or will she be snubbed … Good Lord, I cannot imagine why she must worry so. It seems sometimes that she must dearly enjoy it."

"So you are taking refuge here to avoid her."

"Do not think me so ignoble. I bring with me an invitation."

"Another party?" Pray no, not another! "I am surprised that even you and your sister could manage another one so soon."

"I would be as well. No, it is not another party. I have acquired tickets for the panto, four days from now. When I purchased them, I had every intention of escorting my sister to the theater. But now, I find myself in a quandary. I seem to have planned a very important meeting with the banker that same day. I dare not try to convince him to another date."

If anyone else made such a claim, he would not have believed them. But Bingley … "I cannot fathom how it is you still cannot manage to get your dates straight. You truly must consider hiring a secretary."

"Yes, yes, well, I will pursue that directly come the new year. In the meantime, there is an extra ticket to the panto. Louisa and Hurst are attending—"

"Then Miss Bingley can attend with them, can she not?"

Bingley rubbed the back of his hand along his chin. "Yes and no. She can, but she hates to be gooseberry in such a party. She insists the entire event is a waste if there is no fourth to attend with them. Pray, will you escort her?"

Darcy rose and raked his hair, pacing the room. "You put me in a very disagreeable position, you know."

"I thought you enjoyed the panto."

"I do, that is not the point." Was he really so obtuse?

"Then enlighten me."

"Do you know what happens when I am seen in public, or sometimes even at a private event, with a woman, any woman, who is not related to me?" He stopped in front of Bingley and leveled a stare that should have explained everything.

Bingley offered his characteristic blank gaze and shrugged.

"The gossip begins and, more often than not, it finds its way into the scandal sheets. Speculation begins as to when an offer of marriage might be made and what the terms of the settlement might be."

"Surely you are exaggerating." Bingley laughed.

Contrary man! Darcy glowered; the expression had been known to cow the most stubborn tradesmen and servants, but Bingley hardly blinked. "It is no exaggeration. Even if it were, there is the problem of the lady in question."

"Excuse me?" Bingley pressed his elbows into the arms of the chair and sat very straight.

"If I am in the company of a lady at an event, she inevitably imagines far more interest that I intend. Have you not noticed the care I took in Meryton not to excite the expectations of any young lady?"

How well had those efforts worked? What were Elizabeth's expectations? Did she understand what it meant when he asked her to dance? She was perceptive, surely she did.

Bingley waved off the very notion. "What, Caroline? You must be joking. Caroline has no interest in you. None whatsoever. You are my friend and nothing else."

"I am not so convinced."

"Well, you are wrong. She is not interested in a man who dislikes the pleasures of town and would expect her to remain in the country the better portion of the year. You are entirely safe from her."

Darcy rolled his eyes.

"Did you not see, even last night? She took no great pains to be with you. She exhibited no jealousy when I introduced you to Lady Elizabeth. You have nothing to fear from my sister. If that is your only objection, put your mind at rest and accept the tickets. Go with them, and enjoy yourself. You have been so dour since we left Hertfordshire …" the bright notes left Bingley's voice, and he sighed. "It will be good for you to go."

"It will placate your sister so that you do not have to listen to her continued complaints."

"Well, yes, that too. What say you? I cannot believe you have other engagements at present, and it would be a favor to me."

Darcy grumbled and muttered under his breath. It seemed as though Bingley had been asking many favors of late.

"With Drury Lane not yet rebuilt, this is your chance to see if another can live up to Grimaldi's performance of Clown. You have always wondered if any might be as striking, yet you never opted to see another. How can you ignore so convenient an opportunity?"

Why did Bingley have to look so like his favorite spaniel?

Darcy dragged his hand down his face. "Very well. Thank you for your offer. But I insist on meeting your party at the theater. I will not be seen arriving or leaving with an unmarried woman."

Bingley snorted. "I shall inform Caroline of the conditions of your attendance. She will not be pleased, but she will deem it better than attending alone."

December 28, 1811. Longbourn

Several mornings later, Elizabeth walked with Aunt Gardiner before anyone else had risen. The morning sun framed her face in a halo-like glow as they walked through Mama's rose garden. Only a few roses still struggled to bloom against the winter chill, but they were a reminder that come the warmth of the new year, the place would overflow with an abundance of color and fragrance.

"I do not know how my sister manages it." Aunt Gardiner chuckled under her breath. "We have been here near a week, and not one night have we had a simple family dinner. Last night was the closest we came, and your mother still had what, four additional guests at the table? Boxing Day, two nights ago was the card party, tonight the theatrical at the Goulding's home, tomorrow we are all to dine at the Phillips's. Even talking about the pace your mother keeps is exhausting. We do not go out and about nearly so much when we are at home. I fear that Jane will find us very dull company indeed."

Elizabeth picked a dried blossom off a woody stem, its shriveled petals raining to the ground. "Jane finds great contentment in all things. If you entertain, she will prefer that; if you make calls, she will relish that; if you stay at home, she will pronounce it all very agreeable. I wish I shared her very happy talent."

"It is a happy talent to be rendered content in all circumstances. I give you leave to be envious of it. However, I should wonder if she is choosing to exercise that talent currently. There is something decidedly sad in her eyes, particularly when she thinks no one is looking."

"I do not think it is a problem of her choosing correctly so much as it is Mama's constant reminders that drive her from her place of serenity. It is difficult to set aside being unhappy when you are constantly reminded of being so." Elizabeth kicked a small pile of leaves aside.

"Perhaps you are correct. I do hope a change of scenery will be good for her. I pray your visit to us in the spring shall not take on a similar character."

"Whatever do you mean?"

"All your commendations of Mr. Wickham have left me suspicious as to your mutual attachment. I have been observing you both very closely the last several times you have been in company with one another."

Elizabeth pressed her hand to her cheeks. "What has been the nature of your observations?"

"You are too sensible a girl, Lizzy, to fall in love merely because you are warned against it."

"From you, that is high praise indeed. I shall endeavor not to allow it to overtake my good sense."

Aunt Gardiner paused and turned to catch her gaze. "Seriously, my dear, I would have you be on your guard. Do not involve yourself, or endeavor to involve him, in an affection which the want of fortune would make so very imprudent."

"So then, I am to believe you do not like Mr.

Wickham?" If that were true, she would be the only one in Elizabeth's acquaintance to feel so.

"I have nothing to say against him. He is a most interesting young man. If he had the fortune he ought to have, I should think you could not do better. But as it is—you must not let your fancy run away with you. You have sense, and we all expect you to use it. Your father would depend on your resolution and good conduct, I am sure. You must not disappoint your father."

"My dear aunt, this is being serious indeed." Did Aunt Gardiner believe her mistaken to have refused Mr. Collins?

"Yes, and I hope to engage you to be serious likewise."

"Well, then, you need not be under any alarm. I will take care of myself, and of Mr. Wickham, too. He shall not be in love with me. If, of course, I can prevent it." Elizabeth winked.

"Lizzy! You are not serious now." Aunt laid a hand on her shoulder.

"I beg your pardon. I will try again. At present, I am not in love with Mr. Wickham. But he is, beyond all comparison, the most agreeable man I ever saw—and if he becomes really attached to me—I believe it will be better that he should not. I see the imprudence of it. Oh, that abominable Mr. Darcy!" Elizabeth scuffed the toes of her half-boot into the dirt and kicked a clump of knotted roots. How many lives had Mr. Darcy the privilege of interfering with?

"I am not currently concerned with the character of Mr. Darcy. While I trust your character, I do have concerns about your heart."

A chill breeze rattled the barren rose canes surrounding them.

"My father is partial to Mr. Wickham." Elizabeth turned aside. The eye contact was just too much.

"Partial to Mr. Wickham? I find that rather surprising."

"Even more so, Mama is as well. Shocking, is it not, to find them in agreement about something concerning myself?"

"I find it difficult to believe that your mother is unconcerned as to his lack of fortune." Aunt Gardiner often used that expression when one of her boys was offering her a half-truth.

"She herself suggested that I would be imprudent to ignore his attentions as I have done for a far more eligible gentleman."

"In that choice, I can find no fault. As advantageous as a match to Mr. Collins might have been, it would surely have been your undoing. Mary might have done for him, perhaps even Kitty, but surely not you."

"I cannot tell you how relieved I am to hear you say that. Mama has been so very vexed with me since I acted thus. I had begun to question myself."

"I am troubled to hear that. It would be a shame if you ceased in trusting yourself. We have all a better guide in ourselves, if we would attend to it, than any other person can be." Aunt pulled her shawl a little tighter around her shoulders.

"Thank you. I should be very sorry to be the means of making any of you unhappy. But we see every day, where there is affection, young people are seldom withheld by immediate want of fortune from entering into engagements with each other. How can

I promise to be wiser than so many of my fellow creatures if I am tempted? Moreover, how am I even to know that it would be wisdom to resist? All that I can promise you, therefore, is that I will not be in a hurry to believe myself his first object. When I am in company with him, I will not be wishing it to be so. In short, I will do my best."

Aunt Gardiner sighed, a special disappointed little sound that pinched Elizabeth's heart far more acutely than any of Mama's scoldings ever did. "Perhaps it will also be prudent if you discourage his coming here so very often. At least, you should not remind your mother of inviting him."

"As I did the other day." Elizabeth smiled a little self-consciously. "You are correct. It would be wise to refrain from that. But do not imagine that he is always here so often as he has been recently. It is on your account that he has been so frequently invited. You know my mother's ideas as to the necessity of constant company for her friends. But really, and upon my honor, I will try to do what I think to be wisest; and now, I hope you are satisfied."

"I am indeed. More so, I am relieved that you have not found the need to quarrel or resent me for what I have had to say." Aunt Gardiner returned to the house, but Elizabeth continued on in the garden.

Aunt said she might not do better than Wickham, except for his lack of fortune. Mama thought little of that obstacle. Papa as well. They thought him most agreeable. So did she.

Was it wrong to have hopes for the most agreeable man of her acquaintance?

Why did Aunt's opinion have to be so very different from her parents'? Why did it have to matter to her so much?

She slept fitfully. Between her conversation with Aunt Gardiner and the knowledge that Jane would be leaving with the Gardiners in the morning, Morpheus was kept at bay.

December 29, 1811. Meryton

Elizabeth rose just after dawn. A walk would probably not be very helpful, but she may as well take one. She buttoned her pelisse and snugged her hat just over her ears. That and a warm pair of gloves should keep the early chill at bay well enough.

She slipped into the hall, her half boots whispering along the floor. No sense in disturbing the rest of the house.

"Lizzy?"

Elizabeth jumped. "Jane! What are you doing up?" And already dressed, wearing her pelisse.

She smiled weakly. "I could not sleep either. May I join you?"

"I would relish your company."

They tiptoed down the stairs, nodding to Hill as they ducked out of the kitchen door and into the neat rows of the kitchen garden.

The last of the autumn harvest had been brought in and the air smelt of freshly turned soil, ready for its next plantings. All the weeds had been pulled and the rows straightened, so orderly and tidy, not at all like spring when new bits of green shot up willy-nilly through the dirt and had to be sorted vegetable from weed.

"What disturbed your sleep?" Elizabeth stepped carefully, not to disturb the fresh ground. "You have never been anxious about going to London before."

"I cannot help but think ... is it wrong of me ... I mean I cannot forget that Mr. Bingley is in London. Aunt Gardiner warned me that they go out very little, and they certainly do not mix in the same circles as Mr. Bingley ..."

"You still hold out hope of meeting him there?"

"I know I should not, but I cannot help it. Every time I think I have the thought dispelled from my mind, it returns again with such force it cannot be denied." Jane turned her face up into the golden morning sunlight and bit her lip. "I am a fool, am I not?"

"How can you say such a thing? You are a dear, affectionate creature. That you would be hopeful is little surprising."

"But is it wise, Lizzy? I fear I am only ... no, no, it is foolish. I have determined not to think of him any further, and I will abide by that. I know I shall enjoy the company of my young cousins and my aunt. That and thoughts of you shall be enough for me." Jane dragged a trail with her toes in the soft soil.

"Thoughts of me? Whatever for?"

"I shall think of the pleasant times you must be spending with Mr. Wickham."

"Oh, Jane. In truth I hate to even speak of it now, but you are to leave me soon. I do not know who then I shall be able to talk with. Charlotte has her wedding and new life to plan and things are rather ..."

"Uncomfortable? Awkward?"

"Both. I do not know what to say to her. Such a decision she has made. I do not know how to wish her well without feeling a hypocrite." Elizabeth gazed into the sunrise until its brightness made her squint and turn away.

"She is not you. Be happy in her happiness. That is all you need do."

"But is she happy? Can she be with such a man?"

"Just because you would not does not mean no one can be. Not all can enjoy your good fortune to draw the attention of a man like Mr. Wickham."

"What do you think of him?" Elizabeth bit her lip and held her breath.

"He is everything a young man should be."

"Except rich."

"Have you not said there are not nearly so many wealthy men as there are young women to deserve them?"

"It sounds like something Papa would say. I do not recall saying anything of the kind." But Jane was right, it did sound like something she might say.

"Whomever said it was quite correct. If expecting a man to be wealthy and agreeable and in love with us may be setting the bar far too high, I suppose we must decide, as Charlotte has done, which one of those is most important to us and hope to obtain only that." Jane pursed her lips and looked around. "Do you like him very well?"

"I do not know. I think I do. I very much enjoy spending time in his presence. He seems to seek me out whenever we are in company. I think perhaps that he might like me, too. The thought, I confess, makes me very happy. But do you think it right for me to like him?"

"Right? I do not understand. Do our parents not approve?"

"They both do."

"Then what is your concern? Where there is affection and support from friends and family, then an attachment will doubtless be celebrated and supported." Jane studied her carefully. "Oh, I see. Mama has been so distraught over Mr. Collins and … and Mr. Bingley. You fear seeing her upset once again should this affair with Mr. Wickham come to naught. You are all that is kind and thoughtful."

Was it deceitful not to correct Jane's opinion of her?

"It will be well. I am sure of it. With no opposition on either side and no concerns but his fortune, I am certain that obstacle can be managed. You look so well together, that cannot be for nothing. Promise you will write to me very often and tell of everything. I shall take my joy in yours."

"I think perhaps you think too much of things. He has by no means declared anything to me." The question was, would he? Elizabeth's stomach pinched just a little.

"Then I shall be silent on the matter until you give me leave to speak. But know that in my heart, I shall be awaiting your good news." Jane's smile was ever so hopeful.

"I shall miss you very much whilst you are in London."

"And I you. But knowing how happy you will be here will ease my spirit every time I think of it."

Surely Jane was right. It must be safe to enjoy Mr.

Wickham's friendship. More than safe, it was quite agreeable. She bit her lip to manage the smile that threatened to reveal too much. How lovely it would to be able to please Mama, Papa, herself, and Jane all at once.

Aunt Gardiner would surely reconcile herself to it all when everything worked out as it should.

❧Chapter 7

December 30, 1811. London

THE MORNING OF the panto, Darcy laid his newspaper aside on the parlor sofa, snickering. Miss Bingley should not have worried, her little dinner party hardly garnered any notice from the gossips. A few brief words of Sir Andrew's and Lady Elizabeth's attendance and little more. Would she be gratified at the mention of her event, or offended that it garnered no more notice than a few brief sentences? It was difficult to predict.

No doubt he would find out soon.

The mantle clock chimed, the sound echoing just slightly off the parlor's polished paneling. A little porcelain harlequin all but waved at him from the curio cabinet between the windows. Mother had given it that place of honor because this was the room they gathered in whilst waiting for the right time to leave for the theater. Had he been traveling with his parents, they would have left by now. Mother always had been determined to arrive early when they went to Drury Lane. The crush of people seemed less that way. She knew he found crowds very unsettling.

He still did.

Mother had always been comfortable in a crowd, much like Bingley ... or Miss Elizabeth.

She seemed to know what to say and what to do to make people around her at ease. How did she do that?

The clock chimed the passing of another quarter hour. Procrastination would not make things any easier. He called for his carriage to be brought around.

The ride to the theater passed quickly, too quickly. He scanned the milling crowd for Hurst and Bingley's sisters. Several ladies turned toward him with inquiring glances. They followed his gaze into the crowd, as if trying to discern who he sought. He winced and pinched the bridge of his nose. If only it had been colder, or better, raining heavily, so people would be intent on getting inside, not watching others. But no, it had to be intrusively bright and crisp today.

No, not her!

The woman in the outlandish purple hat with far too many feathers who contributed to the society pages. The hat was new, but the abundance of feathers was the shrew's trademark, appearing in far too many of Darcy's nightmares. No doubt his innocent outing to the panto would be the subject of her pen, probably even tonight.

A white plume bobbed in the crowd, approaching.

Beneath it, Miss Bingley in a dark blue gown and pelisse trimmed with white fur drew near. Behind her, the Hursts hurried to catch up.

"Good afternoon, Mr. Darcy." She and her feather dipped in a small curtsey. "How kind of you to join us."

"I appreciate Bingley's invitation." He did not like to lie, but sometimes it was unavoidable.

"Shall we find our box before any more children arrive?" Hurst cast about the throng, his upper lip pulled back. "Dashed inconvenient thing that these performances draw so many children who should be left in the nursery."

Children often behaved better than their parents once the performance whipped spirits into a frenzy. Young ones rarely incited a riot.

"At least we shall have none in our box." Miss Bingley tapped her fan on her palm.

"You do not like children?" Darcy asked.

"What is to like or not like? They are necessary. That is why nurses and governesses and boarding schools are employed." Miss Bingley shared a knowing glance with her sister.

"Hear, hear," Hurst waved his hand, ducked his chin and waded into the crowd.

Darcy ushered the ladies to follow Hurst and stepped behind to bring up the rear.

It should not bother him that Miss Bingley did not like children. A woman of her rank had little need to. She was entirely correct. Nurses and governesses and tutors could relieve her of nearly all need to interact with any offspring.

His mother had not felt that way about her children, though. How many times had she stolen away into the nursery for the opportunity to read to him from his favorite book? The nurse used to assure her there was no need for the mistress to trouble herself. Still, Mother would not be gainsaid. Sometimes, Father would join her. He would fold himself in a tiny nursery chair to sit with them as she read.

Some of the servants thought the arrangement peculiar, but Mrs. Reynolds would not permit that sort of talk below stairs. He had once overheard her scolding a maid who dared criticize his parents for paying far too much attention to the goings on in the nursery. What man did such a thing?

The kind of man Darcy wanted to be.

But that would require a wife. And more importantly, one who wanted to do more than merely birth her children.

Miss Elizabeth drew children to her. Walking on the streets of Meryton, nursery maids brought their charges to her. Miss Elizabeth would drop to a knee to address them eye to eye. He had never been close enough to hear what they said to her or how she replied. But their laughter and looks of delight said enough. She was not the kind of woman to become a disinterested mother.

"What say you, Mr. Darcy?" Miss Bingley settled herself into the seat beside her sister, in the box high above the crowded lesser seats.

What was she talking about?

"For heaven's sake, Caroline, do not bother the man so. I have no doubt he does not care about the state of Mrs. What's-her-name's daughter's hat." Hurst flipped the tails of his coat out of the way and sat behind his wife. He gestured to the chair beside him.

A flash of purple in the next box over twisted his guts. Did Hurst recognize her, too? He settled himself on the velvet covered chair.

The theater filled, and soon the curtains parted. The crowd hushed, ready to be transported by the magic of the players. He leaned forward, studying the stage. Mother had a remarkable eye for detail. She would whisper in his ear about this bit or that. It had been a game they played: who could discover the most about the details of the stage before the first player came out.

Miss Bingley preferred noticing the details of the other ladies who attended.

Masked characters entered the stage, Cinderella and her father. The masks and costumes were excellent and different to what he had seen before. Definitely distinct from a Drury Lane production.

Miss Bingley pressed her shoulder to her sister's and whispered, "There, in the second-rate seats, the fourth row," she gestured with her chin. "Do you see?"

Were they paying any attention to the production at all?

"I believe I do. In the pink dress? Sitting between the children?" Mrs. Hurst pointed the tip of her finger toward the seats below.

"Yes, yes. Do you think …"

Darcy shifted, leaning on his elbow. Who were they looking at? He peered into the crowd, following their directions.

"Why yes, I think you are right. Oh, Caroline, what are we to do?"

How could they recognize someone by the back of her head, and why ever would it be so significant? Stuff and nonsense!

Darcy leaned back and returned his attention to the pantomime. Harlequin waved the slapstick and the Fairy Queen appeared to change the characters and the setting.

The corner of his lips rose just a mite. As a boy, this was his favorite part of the entire show. There was something innately appealing about such change being so easy and effortless, even if it was just a stage illusion. Masks and outer robes fell away, set pieces turned and tipped and transformed. The world of the harlequinade appeared.

"Here we are again!" Clown cried from the stage and vaulted from one set piece to another.

The children in the audience, especially the youngest ones, jumped to their feet squealing and pointing. The young woman sitting in the fourth row below them turned to speak to the little girls beside her.

A cold wave coursed over Darcy.

Jane Bennet.

She was indeed in London! When had she come, and how long was she to be here? More important, was her sister—the right sister—with her?

Darcy leaned as far forward as he could and peered into the crowd for any sign of Miss Elizabeth. Not that he had any intention of speaking to her. That would surely appear in the society pages. No, any public meeting with her would be impossible. But it would be pleasing to see her, to simply know she was in town.

"She said she had an uncle in Cheapside." Did Mrs. Hurst realize she sounded just like a hissing cat?

"No doubt she is staying with them. I can only guess her intentions are toward continuing her pursuit." If Mrs. Hurst was hissing, Miss Bingley was positively growling.

Cheapside? That was not very far. He could perhaps contrive to walk in that direction ... regularly. No matter if she were in the city, Miss Elizabeth would arrange to take a morning walk, somehow. She was a creature of habit.

But she would not go out alone, a maid, or perhaps her sister, or even the children would accompany her. She might walk out with the nursery maid, or she might even take the task from the maid altogether and entertain the children entirely on her own. Perhaps she would walk with them all the way to Tower Green. The little boys would no doubt enjoy the opportunity to stretch their legs in a good run.

Mother had sometimes taken him there when they stayed at Darcy House. The confinement indoors had been one of the things he least liked about their visits to town.

Tower Green was the kind of place where one might accidentally encounter any number of persons. One might even have a brief conversation, an entirely unremarkable conversation.

What might one say in such an encounter?

A contented murmur rippled through the crowd. Pantaloon placed Columbine's hand in Harlequin's. Cheers rose, all was now as it should be.

At least for Harlequin.

Darcy stood with Hurst and applauded, still searching the crowd for signs of Miss Elizabeth.

After a rousing chorus, to which the audience sang far too many repetitions, the players disappeared off stage. The crowd trickled out of the theater.

Miss Bingley pleaded a dislike of the crush and insisted they remain in their box until much of the theater cleared. Mrs. Hurst agreed, so there was little to be done but wait for their leisure. Perhaps, though, it would be best for him to be seen leaving alone. That could go far in clearing up misunderstandings about the company he kept today. He rose.

"Pray, Mr. Darcy, do not leave us yet." Miss Bingley looked up at him, batting her eyes.

He knew that look far, far too well. Bingley was definitely wrong about his sister's intentions.

"Forgive me, but I must go." He probably should not have come in the first place.

"Wait, I beg of you. There is a matter of very great import which we must discuss." She reached toward him.

He took half a step back. "I have no idea to what you refer."

"Did you not see what we did, there in the audience below us? Jane Bennet."

"I observed a young woman who looked much like Miss Bennet."

"She did not look like Miss Bennet, she was Jane Bennet. I have no doubt whatsoever. Have you already forgotten why we insisted Charles keep to London and eschew his country house?"

In truth, for a moment, he had.

"I fear this is a most serious situation, very serious indeed. You were so integral in convincing Charles to remain in town. I beg your assistance again. We must ensure that he does not become reacquainted with Miss Bennet here in town. I am entirely certain he will not agree to yet another change of venue."

Darcy returned to his seat. "I understand your concern, but I hardly think it likely they should meet by some chance encounter. As I understood, her aunt and uncle are not often in company, and he is in trade. How many opportunities do you have to rub shoulders with tradesmen? No, I think it quite unlikely. You have no reason for concern."

"You underestimate Charles's attachment to Miss Bennet. I have no doubt that should he learn of her being in the city, he will make every attempt to renew his acquaintance."

Was Bingley so very attached? It had not seemed so. But if he was, did that change anything about the situation?

"He well knows the danger such connections might pose to your family's standing. Surely, he could not wish for Mrs. Bennet as a mother-in-law." A shudder snaked down Darcy's spine. What a truly awful fate! That possibility alone should be enough to render any Bennet woman entirely undesirable. And yet ...

The Darcy name and connections were recognized, well able to withstand a ridiculous connection or two. Not at all like the fragility of the Bingley line, so newly established amongst good society.

Miss Bingley fanned her face with her handkerchief. "One would think he had the sense to realize, but I am not entirely sure. We must agree to keep this news amongst ourselves. Charles must not suspect that she might be anywhere nearby."

"I abhor disguise—"

"I understand that, sir, and I hold your character in the greatest of respect. Consider what is at stake, though. Moreover, there is no deception. None at all.

We are merely choosing not to speak, not speaking falsehoods." A thin smile crept over her face, and she blinked a little faster.

The line between the two was very, very fine, perhaps too fine to truly distinguish between. Deception, active or passive, was deception, and as such was an affront to the Darcy character.

So then what was he to do? Should he go out of his way to mention that he had seen Miss Bennet?

No, that would not do either.

"So long as he does not specifically ask if I have encountered Miss Bennet, I will hold my peace." It was an uncomfortable compromise, but it was tolerable.

"I admire your principles, Mr. Darcy. I cannot imagine asking more of you. You are a good friend to my brother. We appreciate the way you are guiding him into society."

"If that is all, then, pray excuse me. Good day." He bowed.

Her features drooped just a mite. "Good day, sir."

He turned and strode out as quickly as he could without breaking into a run. The sooner he left Miss Bingley's presence, and the longer he stayed out of it, the better.

The long, winding staircase was relatively empty. A definite blessing, given his frame of mind. Having to pick through a crowd might have left him running entirely mad.

Outside, he gulped the cooler, crisp air, exactly the balm he needed for Miss Bingley's attentions. Now, to find the coach.

Excellent! His coachman had the carriage waiting exactly where it should be, and he climbed in. Purple-hat-and-feathers had observed his hasty exit from the theater and followed him at a discreet distance. She kept looking over her shoulder, as though she expected to find Miss Bingley trailing after him, or even more dramatic, left somewhere, crying bitter tears in the wake of his rejection.

What a truly vile creature!

Even the possibility of seeing or meeting with Miss Elizabeth hardly outweighed the risk of being subjected to that harpy. He needed to return to Pemberley soon, before the surveillance of the gossips drove him barmy.

But to do so without seeing Miss Elizabeth? That was hardly more acceptable.

He had several more social engagements demanding his presence. Leaving before those would cause more problems than it would solve. Surely he could find out whether Miss Elizabeth was in town during that time.

He would; and then he would leave and be done with the intrigues of the *ton*.

Meryton

The Gardiners departed with Jane early the following morning. The departure of so much good sense and level-headedness immediately made itself felt upon Elizabeth. Papa must have felt it, too. He ensconced himself in his study the whole of the day, only emerging when their departure for the Kings' for a dinner party was imminent.

Mama swept downstairs and into the vestibule, dressed in her best dinner gown and cape, all the while declaring it quite shocking that they should so openly celebrate the death that led to Mary King's inheritance with a dinner party. Papa insisted they were but returning the invitations that had been exchanged earlier in the holiday season. That it happened to coincide with their daughter's good fortune was entirely coincidental.

"You may think that all you like, Mr. Bennet, but I shall not be moved. They mean to remind us all that their daughter is an heiress. I am quite certain they intend to make sure all the attention is upon her. That will only hurt our own girls, you know. How will you like to see their hearts broken when none of the officers pay them any more mind." She dabbed her cheeks with her creased handkerchief.

"I think it very unlikely that any hearts shall be broken, Mrs. Bennet. If they are, then it was a matter of foolishness that they were so attached in the first place. All will be better off for the exercise. Now, to the carriage, unless you would rather stay at home and discuss the point further."

"Oh, Mr. Bennet!" Mama tossed her head and brushed past him on the way out of the front door.

He clutched his forehead and ushered his daughters out.

Lizzy slid into the seat facing Mama. Mary had already established herself near the window. Sitting in the middle was not nearly so trying as sitting knee to knee with Mama.

"You look quite well tonight, Lizzy, but I fear it will do no good. I do not know what has caused such bad luck to befall us, but I fear we are in the thick of it now." Mama reached over to adjust the ribbons on Kitty's skirt.

"Then perhaps, you shall not grumble when we prepare for New Year's Eve." Papa looked just a little too smug. How long had he been waiting to say just that?

"I do not see how that has anything to do with—"

"If we have indeed been plagued with bad luck— and I am by no means agreeing we have—then what better way to usher out the bad luck than by properly observing tradition? A fortuitous first footer on New Year's Day is just the thing we need to turn our fortunes back to good."

Mama huffed and fluffed her feathers, settling into the squabs like broody hen on her nest. "If you insist, I suppose it will do no harm."

"I am most glad to hear you say so. I expect then, you will not feel the need to comment—" He meant complain. "—so vociferously at the necessary efforts."

She huffed again.

"Please, Papa, let us hire another girl to help with the cleaning. You insist on ever so much work to be done." Lydia slumped against the carriage side and threw her head back.

"The effort builds character. If you fear you will be too spent from tonight for the exertion, then return home immediately. Surely this dinner will require too much of you. Perhaps it would be in the interest of good luck for all of us to return home and send the Kings our regrets."

Mama would have sprung to her feet had they not been confined in the carriage. As it was she knocked her knees painfully into Elizabeth's.

"Do not be ridiculous, Mr. Bennet. We can by no means turn around now. How humiliating! How much talk would there be! Surely the Kings would be offended. That might take months to resolve. Lydia, you will be quite well to do whatever your father requires tomorrow, all you girls shall." Her glower added '*is that understood?*'

"Yes, Mama." Lydia pouted.

Kitty mirrored the expression.

Mary opened her mouth to speak but the pressure of Elizabeth's shoulder against hers seemed sufficient to quell the urge. Cold silence descended within. Elizabeth pulled her pelisse a little tighter around her neck. The carriage lurched in a deep rut in the road and nearly pitched her into Mama's lap.

"And you, Lizzy, you must be on your best and brightest behavior tonight. It would not do to have you lose Mr. Wickham's attentions—"

"Oh no! Mama, do not say that! It is not fair that she keeps him to herself. She must let us have our time with him as well," Kitty mumbled into the side glass.

"Indeed, she is right. You must tell her to share him with the rest of us." Lydia stamped and nearly came down on Mary's foot.

"I have no interest in him. She may well have my share of his favors." Mary glared at Lydia.

"Why do we not allow the poor man to choose as he will? Unless, of course, he has come to you, Mrs. Bennet, asking for your assistance in managing his social engagements." Papa peered over his glasses at her, eyebrows raised.

Mama's remark, which would no doubt have been tart and sharp, was cut off by their arrival at the Kings'.

The driver opened the carriage door, and Mama led her daughters out.

"I hope, Lizzy, your mother's ill-humor has not endangered your enjoyment of the evening." Papa straightened his hat.

"No, sir. I am determined to have my share in the fun and frivolity of it."

"That is my girl. Do not worry about your sisters. I have no doubt that such silly girls shall rarely be in want of attention."

Elizabeth swallowed hard. "Of that I am quite sure, sir."

Of course, that attention might not be gracious in its estimation of them, or the family they came from. Pray let there be no opportunity for Mary to play or Lydia to dance tonight.

The liveried butler led them up to the drawing room where Mrs. King pulled herself away from Mama to greet them. She looked a little relieved for the excuse to withdraw. Mama could be a little overwhelming at times.

"Mr. Bennet, Miss Elizabeth, we are so happy you could join us tonight." Mrs. King curtsied. She was a stout, little woman in a voluminous blue print gown many seasons out of style. Still, it was fine quality and complimented Mrs. King's blonde hair and porcelain complexion well. Mama criticized her for her freckles, but they were actually rather pretty, scattered across her nose.

"Your invitation was most propitious. All our company has left us. My wife has found herself quite at loose ends with nothing to distract her." Papa bowed.

Poor Mrs. King, she looked so confused. She had-never been well equipped to deal with Papa's sense of humor.

"I am only sorry that my sister Jane has already gone away to London and is not able to join us."

"Her company will surely be missed. Ah, you will forgive me, the officers have arrived." She slipped away.

"Officers? I had thought your mother exaggerating when she bemoaned their attentions going to Miss King. I thought surely the Kings would not have found their company desirable, apart from that of Colonel Forster, of course."

"Why ever would you think that? They are the most sought after guests this season, at least since the Bingleys have departed." Elizabeth glanced over her shoulder at the milling crowd.

"Not everyone finds the company of the militia desirable. Not all commanders keep their officers in check as Colonel Forster appears to. Pray excuse me. Mr. King is in need of rescue from too much enthusiastic conversation. Why do you not go and join your friends?" He nodded sharply and wandered toward the far side of the room.

Elizabeth shrugged. The sooner the men could have the dining room to themselves, with cigars and port, the happier Papa would be.

Mr. Wickham strode away from Mrs. King and scanned the room. At least she would not want for agreeable company.

She moved toward him. "Good evening, Mr. Wickham."

"Miss Elizabeth, how very charming to see you this evening. How lonely your house must be with all your recent company gone away." He smiled broadly, but his gaze darted about the parlor.

Who was he searching for?

"The house seems very quiet now. We will have to count on the company of our friends to see us through these dark days."

"I cannot imagine how a house filled with so many pretty young ladies could ever encounter dark days. I am entirely certain that Denny and Sanderson shall rise to the occasion quite willingly." He looked over his shoulder. "I think they may have already under-taken the endeavor."

Denny and Sanderson stood in a little knot, with Lydia and Kitty, Maria Lucas and several others, sur-rounding Mary King. Her white gown made her look paler, even a touch sickly. Ginger girls with freckles were not complimented by white muslin.

"What think you of Miss King?" Wickham took a half step toward that group.

"She is a good sort of girl, I think. I have hardly heard a cross word from her in all the time I have known her. She is well-liked among us."

"But you find her dull?"

"I said no such thing." Elizabeth pressed a hand to her chest.

"But the praise you offered her was of the sort that implied exactly that." His eyebrows flashed up.

"You wound me sir. I would by no means offer such censure." Her cheeks heated. Pray no one was looking, or worse, listening in their direction.

"Of course not, you are far too polite. But to praise in so mild terms—what else might I assume?" His right eye twitched in a scant wink.

"That I mean what I say sir, nothing more and surely nothing less." He was being quite playful this evening, but perhaps a touch impolitic, even a little unlike himself.

"That is entirely impossible. Who among us is so plain spoken that they would speak so directly? Shall we join them that I may see for myself this woman whom you condemn with faint praise?" He gestured toward the group of young people in the far corner of the room.

Perhaps it would be best to join them. Staying close to Lydia and Kitty might better keep them in check.

They dodged around chairs and tables, polished and cleaned for the occasion. Perhaps a few too many furnishings had been brought into the room—it was crowded and difficult to navigate. Her toes were trod upon no less than three times before they attained their goal.

The group fell into peals of laughter.

"Such stories, Lt. Denny! I do not think you should be telling such things in polite company." Miss King tittered behind her fan. She was the spit and image of her mother, only tall and slender like her father. But her face, her voice, even the way she misunderstood humor was her mother.

"Oh, but what would the fun in that be?" Lydia leaned her shoulder into Denny's almost as though to remind him she were there.

"A fine question to be sure, Miss Lydia." Wickham intruded half a step into the group.

They shuffled back to accommodate him.

"What amusement might be had that offers no offense to anyone? It is no fine thing to amuse with vulgarities, it has been argued. It requires a superior character to entertain even the most delicate of ears.

Only the finest among us might rise to that challenge." Wickham bowed with a flourish.

"I quite agree, sir." Miss King edged a little closer to Wickham.

"So then, I issue a challenge to you, my fellow officers and other gentlemen. Let us entertain the good ladies here tonight with an overwhelming show of taste and good breeding."

Nods and approving grunts issued from the gentlemen, although a few looked less pleased than Wickham over the arrangement. Maria Lucas clapped softly, encouraging the ladies to do likewise.

"Let us add just a small bit of sport to this. Miss King, would you be so good as to judge tonight whom you find the most pleasing. A bit of competition has always been known to bring out the best in gentlemen."

"And what should the prize to the winner be?" Young Mr. Goulding called from the back of the group.

"A prize, yes a prize…" Wickham paced two steps forward and back, stroking his chin.

"You cannot have a contest without some prize or forfeit." Lydia batted her eyes.

"Indeed you are correct, Miss Lydia. Since the evening is in your honor Miss King, I say the prize should come from you. Would you favor the winner, with, let us say, two dances?"

Miss King giggled. "I should be quite honored. But who shall play for us?" She cast a quick glance toward Mary, her lip barely curled in a sneer.

Not Mary! Pray, not her! How ungracious to seal her good fortune by showcasing another's flaws. Thoughtless and small-minded.

Wickham turned to Elizabeth and bowed. "Miss Bennet, would you be so good as to favor us with your playing at the conclusion of our challenge?"

"I … ah … certainly, I would be pleased to oblige, but I do not know that my talent is sufficient to the task."

Miss King brightened visibly. "Not at all, you play delightfully. You must play Lord Byron's Maggot for us. I declare it is quite my favorite dance."

Of course that would be her request. What better opportunity to showcase her flirting skills, and her triumph over the other girls, than with that particular dance?

"May we prevail upon you for that favor?" Something about the way Wickham looked at her made it impossible to refuse him.

Mrs. King broke into the group. "Ladies, shall we to dinner now?"

Wickham offered Miss King his arm and followed Mrs. King. The other officers and young men did likewise until Elizabeth was left alone watching the others depart for the dining room.

That there should be gentlemen unequal to the number of ladies in the room was not at all unusual. But to be the one left without an escort was a far more infrequent and uncomfortable occurrence. She had anticipated Mr. Wickham would escort her, but it was Mary King's night after all.

Still though …

Best not dwell too much upon it. She followed the rest to the dining room.

The young people clustered together near the center of the table and provided merry conversation. Mr.

Wickham deviated from proper decorum, not limiting his talk to Mary King on his left or Miss Goulding on his right, but addressing all who were easily within hearing. As he was easily the most diverting man at the table, no one complained at his rudeness for the general amusement offered them all.

How ironic that such a breach in propriety would make the young gentlemen's attempts at propriety so very entertaining.

Across the table, Denny could be quite clever when he chose to exert himself. Sanderson's wit proved somewhat wanting, but he too improved himself with the effort to ape Wickham. Young Mr. Goulding said little, but he clearly made himself a student of the exercise. His quick eyes followed the banter, likely cataloguing it for future use. Wickham seemed to notice and flourish under all the attention, rising to the occasion, providing an exemplar of how to well-please his company.

All told, dinner proved exceedingly agreeable, even if she had been largely left out of the fast moving conversations. One tiny question nagged, worrying at her good spirits like a horsefly in summer. Why had Mr. Wickham chosen this evening to demonstrate such exceedingly good manners?

At the end of the sweet course, Mrs. King escorted the ladies to the drawing room. Mary was asked to favor them on the pianoforte. No doubt she would enjoy the opportunity to display. But, at least this way Mary might make a spectacle of herself to only half as large an audience.

The other young ladies gathered at the far end of the room, leaving Mrs. King and her peers the seats nearer the fire.

Miss Goulding leaned forward and glanced back at the matrons. "I cannot believe how entertaining the gentlemen are tonight. Are these the same ones we have kept company with so many times before?"

"It is an impressive transformation, is it not?" Miss King tittered again.

Would that she would stop that stupid, insipid expression.

"What a good leader Mr. Wickham is," Lydia said. "See how he has improved them all. I should think he will become a captain soon."

That was not how militia rank worked. Elizabeth bit her lip. Correcting Lydia in public never went well.

"I think I shall thank him for the improvement he has wrought in our society," Miss Goulding declared.

"Oh yes, I think we all must do so. How shall we best express our appreciation?" Miss King's question should have been mild enough, but there was something vaguely bitter in her tone.

Elizabeth rose and left the others to decide best on how to thank Mr. Wickham. She wandered to a bookshelf and picked up a book left open, a bit of poetry, bemoaning the foolishness of youth and love.

"You would not prefer reading to cards, would you, Miss Elizabeth?" Young Mr. Goulding said, peeking over her shoulder.

She jumped and shut the book. "Oh, I did not hear you come in."

"Would you care to join us at cards? There is a table for commerce forming now." He gestured toward the center of the room.

Wickham shuffled cards, Mary King to his left, Lydia to his right, chatting contentedly with both.

Lydia certainly could not complain that Elizabeth

was taking an unfair share of Mr. Wickham's attention tonight.

"I should like to join you." She followed him to the table.

The play was lively, with great good humor shared throughout, but not once did Mr. Wickham look at her. When they game ended, the players left to help themselves to trays of newly arrived refreshments. Wickham lingered behind a moment to arrange the cards and tokens.

"Are you enjoying this evening, sir?" Elizabeth asked.

"Indeed I am. What is there not to enjoy with such good company and so many amusements at hand?"

"This time of year the amusements are many are they not? My father has already set his mind on preparing the house for a New Year's first footer."

"Indeed that is a most agreeable custom. I believe not so many participate in it so far south."

"I think that is true, but he sees to it that the tradition is maintained."

"How interesting. Pray excuse me. Our hostess is demanding my company. I am loath to disappoint her." He dipped his head and sauntered off to Miss King.

He was right. He did owe her special courtesy, particularly if he was to win his bet. Surely a dance with Miss King could not be so valuable, could it? His standing among the other gentlemen, though, was.

Of course, it must be so.

The notion became harder to believe when Elizabeth took to the piano to play the promised dances. Mr. Wickham looked so very pleased to take Miss King's hand to lead her in the dance. Far more pleased than if he had merely been saving face among the other officers. He led Mary away from the dance, toward the pianoforte. For a moment it looked as though he might speak to Elizabeth, but at the last moment he turned away from her without a second glance.

It was not a cut, no not at all. But then, why did it feel like one?

Soon after, the carriages were summoned and Lydia squeezed in between Elizabeth and Mary.

"I say that was a fun evening, with all the gentlemen trying so hard to be agreeable and pleasing. See what happens when you stop holding Mr. Wickham's attentions all to yourself. The whole party was made so happy." Lydia smiled so smugly.

Elizabeth pressed her lips tight to contain the tart remark that hovered on the tip of her tongue. Several glasses of wine had left Mama quiet and restful. There was little point in disrupting the bit of peace that offered. Besides, it seemed petty and jealous to be so unsettled by one evening without Wickham's devoted attentions.

Surely he still liked her very well. What possible reason was there for her to have fallen in his regard?

.

❦Chapter 8

December 31, 1811 London

THE NEXT DAY Darcy arose, more settled and at peace in himself than he had been in weeks. Today he had a purpose, a plan, an intention, a question that must be answered. Why that should be so soothing escaped him, it was enough that it was.

After a cursory check of the previous day's post and a bite to eat, he set out. The air was bracing, even a mite cold, but in a healthy, invigorating sort of way, reminding him of his own vigor and strength. The long walk would be a welcome opportunity for contemplation and allow him to avoid the notice that the use of his carriage always drew.

Why risk a visit to Cheapside drawing unnecessary attention?

Perhaps, he was being overly cautious. Perhaps, he

was far too concerned with what others said about him. Perhaps, it was just his pride grown out of control. All those things were possible, but none were compelling reasons to act any differently.

There was something pleasant about the sharp morning air and getting lost amidst the dense buildings and burgeoning crowds traversing the streets, a strange sense of being an unremarkable part of something larger than himself. Simply not being gawked at was pleasing.

The crowd grew denser as he approached Cheapside. It moved at its own pace, entirely oblivious to the desires of the individual, ebbing and flowing like the waters of the ocean, to its own primal tempo. Trickles ran through the alleys. Groups of shoppers, like sea foam, caught temporarily against the splendidly bedecked shop windows, then splashed away.

A wave held him lingering at a confectioner's window, displaying Twelfth Night cakes topped with fantastical sugar structures. He might have chosen to loiter there a moment himself. Mother always featured cakes like those at her spectacular Twelfth Night balls. Though he had been too young to attend those balls, she had always permitted him to view the cake whilst it sat in the kitchen, waiting for the ball. She and Mrs. Reynolds always secreted away a piece for him, to be served with his breakfast the next day, with a dainty sugar-work figure to accompany it.

A little sugar-woman on the front-most cake, holding her skirt as if to dance, caught his attention. Something in the figure's posture, perhaps it was the turn of its head, spoke of Miss Elizabeth. Chin held high, almost impertinent, it seemed to beckon others to join in the dance, just as she had at the Netherfield ball.

He shook his head sharply as his heart beat a little faster.

Forcing himself away from the confectioner's window, he allowed himself to be caught in the tide of shoppers, pulled back into the main flow. From the corner of his eye, he saw it. *Gardiner's Fine Fabrics* painted in elegant letters on the second story brick face. A white sign hung above the door bearing the same moniker in gold letters. Beside the name, a skillfully drawn silhouette of a wigged man holding a length of fabric.

The flow of the crowd tossed him onto the shop's front steps. He edged back slightly to peer into the shop windows. Lengths of fine silks, linens and even some printed muslins hung in flowing swirls and puddles, intertwined with all manner of trims and feathers.

Even the linen drapers Georgiana favored would be hard-pressed to match the artistry of this display. Here was a shopkeeper who attended to every detail of his business, the kind of man he most respected.

He inched toward the door, but could not move further until the current caught him up again and swept him inside with several society matrons. The warmth of many bodies filled the space. The scents of linen and silk hung on the air, mingled with fresh flowers and expensive perfumes. Customers lined the walls admiring displays that rivaled the shop window and milled around tables bearing more goods carefully placed in the middle of the room.

"Now, you must promise me not to breathe a word of this place back in Mayfair," a woman with a large matching muff and tippet whispered loudly to the woman beside her.

"You have my word, dear, you have my word," her companion, wearing an over-large woman's shako adorned with a sheer scarf and far too many feathers, replied.

"Not a week goes by without someone asking me where I have come by this muslin or that silk, but I never tell them." Muff-and-tippets tittered into her hand.

Good thing for Gardiner that not all his customers avowed the need for such secrecy. To the contrary, the press in the shop suggested word had spread quite well.

At least four young men—no, six—all neat and smartly dressed, dashed back and forth behind the counters attending to clients. Another younger boy appeared, breathless from the back room. He pulled open a drawer behind the counter, removed several bundles of ribbon and sprinted away.

Was that the sound of someone running up a staircase? How many more customers were upstairs?

"Mr. Gardiner!" Muff-and-tippets extended her hands and cut a swath through the crowd, approaching a well-dressed, well-looking man.

Darcy studied him from the corner of his eye. His smile, his eyes, the line of his jaw, all bore a strong resemblance to Mrs. Bennet, but an even stronger one to Miss Elizabeth.

No doubt he was in the right place. He steeled himself for the vulgarity that must surely come next from any relation to Mrs. Bennet.

"Good day, madam. It is so lovely to see you here." He bowed.

"May I present my favorite linen draper, Mr. Gardiner," she gestured to Shako-and-feathers.

"A pleasure to make your acquaintance."

She was introducing a tradesman to her friend as if he were a gentleman. Darcy's eyes widened, and he forced himself not to stare.

Gardiner's manners were impeccable and his style as gracious as any man welcoming a guest into his home. Nothing like the smooth, slippery air of most shopkeepers and sellers of goods. If it were possible for a gentleman to keep shop, that was exactly what he was seeing.

So, Miss Elizabeth had relations who were quite tolerable and even respectable. He sucked in a deep breath and exhaled slowly. That was a very good thing indeed.

He tugged his coat and found his way into the flow trickling out of the door.

Outside, he pressed himself against the building's front wall to avoid being swept up into the current once more. No doubt the Gardiners did not live above the shop as most shopkeepers did. Where might he find them?

He slipped into the alleyway next to the shop and stood just beyond the pull of the throng. He could not ask directly, but there must be some way.

A side door swung open and the young, running boy from the shop tumbled out.

"I'll get this to missus and bring back her answer directly." He shut the door and pulled his cap a little tighter down over his ears.

The boy dashed passed Darcy. He waited just a heartbeat and followed. The dense multitudes proved his allies, slowing the boy's progress and allowing him to follow without being obvious. There was every chance the boy was not going to the Gardiners' house. Following him might end up on some unsavory street … No, he would not follow so blindly. He had some modicum of sense and dignity left to him.

The boy led him just a few streets away, to a rank of second-rate townhouses, neat and well-kept. He scampered up to the door of the central house, the largest of the set, and knocked. The housekeeper admitted him immediately.

Was this the Gardiners' home? The paint was fresh and it looked like the elegant, scrolling ironwork was a new addition. It was certainly an acceptable abode.

A flash of movement caught his eye. A woman with several children and their nursery maid approached. Could it be Miss Elizabeth?

He crossed the street and turned his back. She could not recognize him, not now. A hack chaise waiting in front of one of the townhouses offered cover. He ducked behind it, peeking out to watch the parade.

The woman was familiar, very familiar, but it was as Miss Bingley had declared, Miss Jane Bennet, not her sister. She led the children and the maid into the house.

He huffed loudly and the horse chuffed in response. Darcy strode back across the street. He reached into his pocket, found a tuppence and rubbed it between his fingers until it warmed to body temperature.

The front door opened again, and the boy reappeared. He bowed once, mumbled something, and scurried down the front steps.

As he passed, Darcy matched his pace and walked with him. "You work for Mr. Gardiner?"

"Aye, sir."

"And that is his home?"

"Why do you want to know that? I … I ain't gonna tell you nothing that might hurt him. Mr. Gardiner is a good master, and I won't be letting—"

"You concern is very admirable and speaks well of both you and of him. I have no desire to harm him or his family. I became acquainted with some of his family whilst in the country."

"One of his nieces stays with him now. You are wanting to call upon her, sir?" The boy stopped and looked up at him.

Darcy started. "Ah, no, nothing so forward. I … I had thought to leave my card perhaps, but wanted to ensure I had the correct direction first."

"And have you the direction correct, sir?"

"I … I do not think so. The man you describe is far different to the one I expected to find. Here, for your trouble." He pressed the coin into the boy's hand and strode away.

He avoided Cheapside on the long walk back to his townhouse.

She was not here.

Elizabeth was not here.

Any sensible man would be relieved. The complication had been avoided, and he was safe.

But perhaps he was no longer sensible. Perhaps he had not been since he had met her.

A little sliver of cold slid along his ribs, toward the center of his chest, a bit like the one that had been lodged there since his mother's passing.

He swallowed hard. No, this was for the best.

The housekeeper anticipated his arrival with hot water ready for tea. She brought a tray into his office and made a hasty retreat. She had worked for him long enough to recognize the expression he wore without him saying a word.

He fell into his leather wingback and threw his head back into the familiar worn depression in the stuffing. Father had worn it into the chair before him. Mother had often laughed at how similar he and his father were. But had father ever chased a woman, who was not even there, to an unfamiliar house? Had he spied upon a shopkeeper, followed his boy, not even knowing where he went?

Surely not!

Certainly not!

Father would be appalled at Darcy's behavior, with very good reason.

Darcy sprang to his feet and stalked across the room and back again. What had become of him? Even Bingley would be hard-pressed to rival the foolishness Darcy had just displayed.

This could not continue; it must not!

He fell back into his chair and snatched up the paper that the housekeeper had left tidily folded on the tea tray. The newspaper made a satisfying snap as he flipped it open. News of parliament and the war, prices, taxes, trade goods. None of it caught his attention. But his gaze locked upon the society pages.

He grumbled under his breath. Only fools read the drivel contained on those pages.

Fools and himself.

Scanning the columns for familiar names, he held his breath and clenched his teeth.

Dash it all! Bloody damnation!

Purple-hat had indeed taken her pen in hand after the panto. There in black and white, she speculated on the company he kept and confusing behaviors he exhibited toward a certain young lady he sat near at the theater, but neither arrived nor left with. What could it mean? Perhaps that he was still declaring himself free and available, or perhaps there was a secret amour covered by such casual contact.

Snarling, he crushed the paper into a ball. He stomped to the fireplace and shoved it in, taking up the poker to feed it directly into the flames.

The spleen, the audacity! How dare she speculate about his private intentions! Exactly as he had warned Bingley, no movement of Darcy's was safe from the gossips. What great good fortune Elizabeth was not in town. What disaster might have arisen from even a casual conversation with her?

How close had even today's ill-considered actions brought him to an untoward exposure to a poisoned pen? He braced his shoulder on the mantel and panted. This was not to be borne.

No, more! All thoughts of Elizabeth, all musings and pleasant considerations had to stop now. It was far too dangerous.

The resolution should have brought him peace. Indeed, what other possible outcome could it have? But somehow, the determination not to think of her only fueled the tormenting thoughts further. At last his port decanter proved the only means by which he might silence them.

He drank and paced and paced and drank. Near midnight, his feet dragged heavily against the marble, and he leaned against the wall for support.

The case clock chimed twelve times. The end of the old year.

Darcy staggered to the front door and opened it to usher in the new year. A cold breeze blasted his face, rousing his muzzy faculties.

"May you, 1812, bring me better fortune than 1811," he muttered, shuffling toward the back door, to conduct out the bad luck that had brought Elizabeth Bennet across his path.

Meryton

On New Year's Eve, Papa wasted no time in arranging for his very specific wishes to be fulfilled. Ashes, rags, scraps and all things perishable had to be removed from the house. The principal rooms required a thorough cleaning.

Hill, Cook and the maid all hated New Year's Eve in equal measures. Mama probably hated it most of all. The volume of work to be done required that she and all her daughters join in the efforts, something she assiduously tried to avoid.

Usually Jane and Elizabeth would work together and reminisce over the events of the past year. Jane had such an excellent memory, particularly for those things pleasant and agreeable. Elizabeth's contributions tended toward the ridiculous. Together, they made short work of the chores at hand.

This year, Elizabeth had no such relief. Whilst Mary proved an efficient and hardworking partner, her conversation was limited to observations on the moral value of hard work and the suggestions of Mrs. Rundell's book in how best to accomplish it.

Elizabeth favored her with the appropriate utterances of attention, but turned her own focus inward as she spread damp, used tea leaves along the floor and swept the parlor.

She had never anticipated a first footer's arrival as she did this night's. Would Mr. Wickham act on her suggestion? Did he even recognize it for what it was? She could not come out and ask; that would be improper and violate the spirit of Papa's traditions. If only she could, though.

Even if he came, would he give her any indication of what had happened the previous night, why he was so distant? Was it some passing oddness of that particular evening, or had something truly changed? Surely, she could not have been imagining his favor before, had she?

No, fretting would do no good and change nothing. But the flutterings in her stomach made it so natural and easy to do. Was this how Mama felt when she complained about her nerves? Heavens, pray that was not the case. To have nerves like Mama and not yet be one and twenty!

Enough of that! Thank heavens there was still plenty of work to focus upon!

Mary got her attention, and they retrieved the carpet from the outside line where Mrs. Reynolds and the maid had been beating it. It took several tries to get it lined up the way Mama preferred, but at last, the carpet was back in place. They would soon be finished with the parlor.

She unpinned the drapes, allowing them to puddle down to the now very clean floor. Why should Mr. Wickham and his attention to Mary King bother her so? It was not as if she fancied herself in love with

MARIA GRACE

him, violently or otherwise. He was an agreeable gentlemen, granted the most agreeable of her acquaintance, but nothing more.

Yet, she did like him. Very well. Very well indeed. As did Mama and Papa.

Oh bother! All this wondering and worrying sounded far more like Lydia than herself. How very vexing!

She flipped out her dust cloth and sneezed. How very considerate of Papa to ensure she could occupy her mind for the rest of the afternoon with cleaning the drawing room.

"Hurry along now, hurry along." Papa ushered Kitty and Lydia ahead of him as he trudged down the stairs and into the parlor, exactly the same as he had done last year and the year before and the one before that.

Elizabeth turned aside and bit the inside of her cheek. Mama would scold if she sniggered aloud. Proper young ladies did not laugh in company, particularly when Mama was irritable.

Jane would have shared a private laugh with her when they finally tucked into bed. But she was off to London. Only a day gone and already she was sorely missed.

"You have had the maid remove all the ashes?" Papa pulled chairs toward the center of the room, into a rough circle.

Candlelight filled the dark corners, turning the summer garden feel of the room into something more reminiscent of an autumn bonfire. Warm and cozy and friendly.

Mama flipped her skirts and settled into a seat.

"Yes, yes and Hill has given all the kitchen scraps away as well. I dare say your pointers are very happy tonight."

"Capital, capital." Papa nudged a final chair into place.

He asked the same questions every year. There was something comforting in his predictability even if Mama disliked it.

"Truly Mr. Bennet, I do not understand why you insist upon this—"

"Do not say foolishness, Mrs. Bennet." He raised a warning finger.

She arranged the fringe on her shawl. "It is naught but superstition and nonsense."

Not unlike puddings and charms.

"Shall I remind you how you recently complained of bad luck? Moreover, I endure your endless talk of lace and frippery. One evening of the year, it is not too much to ask of you—"

Mama folded her arms over her chest and harrumphed. "When you put it in those terms—"

"It is very nearly midnight," Kitty pointed at the clock.

They all turned toward the venerable longcase clock in the corner, its hands nearly overlapped below the '12'.

Papa rose and hurried to the front door. The clock struck the first chime of midnight, and he opened the door. "Welcome to the Year of Our Lord eighteen twelve. Now to usher out eighteen eleven." He tromped through the hall to the back door. It creaked in protest and thumped against the wall like it always did when fully opened.

A sharp breeze whistled from the front door. Not

just sharp, but nearly icy! Elizabeth rubbed her hands up and down her upper arms. Somehow, New Year's Eve always managed to be windy, at least at midnight if no other time.

"Do hurry along Mr. Bennet, or we shall catch our deaths." Mama knotted her shawl around her shoulders more tightly.

Papa waved her down as he passed through the parlor with his particular, heavy-footed gait and shut the front door. A moment later and the backdoor was shut as well and the cold drafts ceased.

"What now, Papa?" Kitty asked.

"I am sure we will have to sit here waiting until someone comes to the door." Mama frowned and shook her head as though she had drunk sour milk.

"I propose a game of spillikins to pass the time." Papa retrieved the game from the cabinet while Kitty and Lydia moved a small table into the center of the chairs.

For a man with large hands, Papa was surprisingly good at the game, but Mama's nimble fingers gave her a distinct advantage at retrieving the tiny ivory sticks without disturbing the rest of the pile. Lydia lacked the patience to be very good at it, though she found her amusement in teasing the rest when they fumbled. It proved an excellent distraction whilst they waited for—

The front door creaked open and Hill muttered something she could not make out.

"Halloo there—is a first footer wanted here?"

Surely that could not be … Elizabeth rose, her heart racing, but Lydia and Kitty preceded her to the front door.

"Mr. Wickham!" Lydia squealed and shouldered Kitty out of her way.

Was it only coincidence or had he correctly divined her invitation? Her chest ached, and she bit her lip waiting for sight of him.

"Come in, come in." Papa ushered Mr. Wickham in and shut the door.

"A tall, dark and handsome man is the best first footer." Lydia clung to Mr. Wickham's right arm.

"But only if water will run under his foot." Kitty clutched his left elbow.

They half escorted, half dragged him to the parlor. He glanced at Elizabeth, who remained several steps behind them. His eyes twinkled with good humor. Did he wish rescue from Kitty and Lydia, or was he enjoying their attentions? She had always been certain of the former before, but now—she was not so sure.

"Sit down, Mr. Wickham and let us see your feet." Lydia shoved a chair at him.

"You will find them very acceptable, Miss Lydia."

Kitty pulled his arm, and he stumbled into a seat.

"I believe we can take one of His Majesty's officers at his word regarding the shape of his feet." Papa leveled a stern gaze upon them lest they start wrestling with Mr. Wickham's boots.

"Besides, I believe it is equally significant that he does not arrive empty-handed." Elizabeth cocked her head and quirked her brow.

Mary donned an attitude of boredom, still as taciturn and broody as she had been through most of their efforts cleaning. Was she still upset over Mr. Collins? Did she still have to be so sensitive, even over the attentions of young men she did not especially like?

Mama leaned toward Elizabeth. "Do not be so rude. Mr. Wickham is welcome regardless—"

"No, Lizzy is right. It is a bad omen indeed for a first footer to arrive empty handed." Papa wagged his finger at Mr. Wickham who winked.

"Never fear, my gracious hosts! I have come well-prepared for the evening." He reached into the market bag slung over his shoulder. "Let me see now, here is a coin." He handed it to Mama with a bow. It was just a penny—not a silver coin as it more properly should have been—but it was enough.

She giggled as she took it.

"And a bit of whisky." He passed a flask to Papa. "Sweets for two young ladies." He handed Lydia a piece of shortbread and Kitty a small black bun.

He must have visited Papa's favorite baker in town. That was the only place one could acquire a black bun in Meryton. Elizabeth ran her knuckles along her lips. What could such diligence mean?

"And Miss Mary." He handed her a small paper packet. "For you, salt, replete with symbolism you best appreciate."

She took it, a little light returning to her eyes.

He turned to Elizabeth. "I fear all I have left for you is this." He held up a lump of coal.

What a charmingly useful gift. Useful, dirty and drab.

She forced a smile and took the coal. He avoided her gaze as she took it from his hand.

"Lead him through the house and demonstrate the excellent work of your mother's staff. Then we may warm his welcome by putting the coal on the fire." Papa gestured toward the hall door.

"Mr. Wickham does not need to see the house is clean." Mama sniffed.

"And I am sure he would much rather a toast than put coal on the fire." Lydia donned a well-practiced pout.

"At the right time, my girl." Papa twitched his head toward the door. "There is an order to these things that must not be forsaken."

"Indeed." Mr. Wickham extended a hand toward Kitty and Lydia, turning his shoulder to Elizabeth. "Perhaps you will do me the favor of escorting me through the house."

They immediately took his arms, giggling. Lydia snuck a smug glance at Elizabeth. Their footsteps echoed on the clean floors as they disappeared down the corridor.

Papa lifted his eyebrows at Elizabeth.

She shrugged and turned away, pulling her shawl a little more tightly around her shoulders. No, she was not going to trail after them, fighting with Kitty and Lydia for a place with the first footer. She shivered. When would he close the doors and put a stop to the cold breezes tearing through the house?

Giggles and loud whispers announced their return.

"Have you found the house to your discerning standards?" Papa asked.

"Cleaner than even my grandmother could desire."

"Shall we all to the parlor where I have poured a toast." Papa pressed the dull steel flask into Wickham's hand. "Your gift is most appreciated, but my ladies are not accustomed to the rigors of whisky. You and I may so indulge, but wine is far more to their sensibilities."

Wickham tucked the flask into his coat with a

wink. "Of course you are right, and very gracious of you to make it so."

They followed Papa back to the parlor, Wickham close to his side. On his heels, Kitty and Lydia jostled to be in his shadow.

No sooner did they step into the parlor than Papa pressed a glass into her hand. "Add the coal to the fire, Lizzy dear, and we shall have a toast."

"Hurry up, must you always take so long at everything?" Lydia edged her out of the way and looped her arm in Wickham's.

Elizabeth tossed the coal into the fire. "And so we shall have warmth in the coming year."

The fire popped and flickered and felt so very cold.

"To Longbourn and all who dwell within." Wickham raised his glass. "May the welcomes continue to be warm, the table full and filled with flavor and prosperity."

They all sipped their glasses.

"If I may have the privilege, sir?" Wickham placed his glass on the mantle.

"It is your right." Papa gestured at Mama.

She offered her hand. Wickham brought it to his lips as she tittered like a girl.

Lydia edged closer, but he turned toward Mary and extended his hand.

Her cheeks flushed, and she muttered sounds that resembled protests, but she extended her hand toward him. He kissed it with the same ceremony he had Mama's, and she flushed deep crimson.

Lydia and Kitty jostled for the position nearest him and presented their cheeks. Wickham smiled, eyes twinkling, and placed a kiss on each of their cheeks. As one, they sighed and pressed a hand to their cheeks. Such silly girls. Perhaps, Papa had not exaggerated when he called them the silliest girls in all England.

Elizabeth fought not to roll her eyes. She turned aside and into Mr. Wickham's shoulder. He stepped back, and for the first time in their acquaintance, looked bewildered.

She cocked her head and raised an eyebrow.

He looked away.

Something inside her shattered like a glass knocked from the mantle.

"Will you stay a little longer, or do you care to usher out last year's troubles and sorrows with you?" Papa gestured toward the back of the house. "I imagine first footers are welcome in many houses tonight."

"You have been as gracious as the Kings were, but I would not overstay my welcome. Lead the way. Ladies." Mr. Wickham bowed and followed Papa out.

The backdoor swung shut. No doubt Wickham would be off in search of another house in want of a first footer. After all, he had already been to other house. He had been to see the Kings.

Mary King. And her new fortune—his first priority.

She sank into a faded velvet armchair and pinched the bridge of her nose. Papa had been right, he had done the job quite credibly. Hopefully Papa would not gloat.

❧Chapter 9

January 5, 1812. London

THE FIRST FIVE days of 1812 offered moments of
solace, punctuated with flashes of torment. Leaving
off all thoughts of Elizabeth left him muttering and
pacing. Nightmares plagued him, leaving him as sleep-
less as an opium eater deprived of his poppies. The
worst of it he kept at bay by diving into his work.
Pemberley's farms and fields would benefit much
from his frenzied studies of the latest techniques in
farming and drainage. But every venture beyond the
confines of his sanctum brought fresh waves of irrita-
tion. Everything called her to mind, sometimes subtly,
sometimes with poignant clarity, but always returning
to thoughts of her.

The afternoon sunlight tumbled through the windows, laying a neatly ordered path of light through his study, illuminating everything the way he best liked it. Yet, even the well-arranged room, the books that lined up just so on the shelves, the neat stacks of work on his desk, not a page out of place, none of those things soothed his soul as they usually did.

Darcy paced across the front of his desk, eyes never leaving the taunting bit of stationary. Lady Matlock's elegant hand plagued him with an invitation to her Twelfth Night ball.

The missive arrived the day after his return from Meryton, when his thoughts were still well-ordered and his to command. He had immediately sent his promise to attend. The act had been automatic, a reflex of politeness, bred into him by a long line of proper, well-mannered Darcys. Had he but taken a few moments to consider his actions ... but no, even if he had, he could never have foreseen his current state of agitation.

Under the best of circumstances, he dreaded balls. This one in particular, he loathed with a fire reserved for all things pretentious and social.

He did not perform well to strangers. This ball would be naught but an extended performance to many strangers. He might as well be a circus animal—a wise pig or a counting horse—put through his paces for the peeresses and heiresses by ring master Lady Matlock.

The only lady he had any desire to perform for ...

No! She would not occupy his thoughts now. The port decanter caught a glint of sunlight and tipped its hat at him from across the room. What an excellent notion.

The housekeeper's knock stopped him mid-step.

Dash it all!

He squeezed his eyes shut. It was too early in the day to seek solace from port in any case. "Come."

She peeked in and dropped a small curtsey. "Colonel Fitzwilliam to see you, sir. Are you home to him?"

"Show him in." How could Fitzwilliam have known how little he wanted company at present? His timing was remarkable that way.

Darcy tugged his coat straight and hurried into a chair near the fire. No point in giving Fitzwilliam the satisfaction of seeing evidence of his discomfiture.

"Good afternoon, Darcy." Fitzwilliam sauntered in, relaxed and informal, as though this were his own home.

How did he do it? Fitzwilliam seemed at home wherever he went and never met a stranger. Whether on the street or at a ball, people thronged to make his acquaintance.

"Good afternoon." Darcy rose and offered a small bow. Still probably too formal for the occasion, but it was the most comfortable greeting he knew. "To what do I owe the pleasure of your company?"

Fitzwilliam extended his hand and would not withdraw it until Darcy shook it. Yes, their relationship did permit such familiar gestures, but was it necessary to exercise them at every encounter?

"Do try to relax, Darcy. We are family after all." Fitzwilliam sank into his favorite chair and balanced one foot upon the other.

Had he any idea of his appalling posture? What a dreadful picture he painted of one of His Majesty's officers.

"You may thank my mother for the call."

Darcy clutched his temples. "Dare I ask her purposes?"

"Probably not, but I will tell you all the same." Fitzwilliam laced his hands behind his head and sniggered. "She instructs me to ensure your attendance at her ball."

"I already sent—"

"I know—I saw the response myself—she showed it to me to scold my penmanship. Excellent hand you have, by the bye, most elegant."

"And that is not enough for her?"

"You know how fastidious she is, and she knows how you would rather break your own leg than attend."

"You think I would manufacture a fall down the stairs to avoid the ball?"

"Not I." Fitzwilliam touched his chest and shook his head. "But my mother is an entirely different matter."

Darcy stared at the ceiling and muttered under his breath.

"Truly, I do not understand your aversion to—"

"Donning a costume—worse yet, one not of my own choosing?" Darcy strode to Fitzwilliam and towered over him.

"Must you always make the worst of everything? I will have you know, Mother selected your character very carefully. Brooded over it for days, lest it keep you from attending. I am instructed to inform you that there will be no random draw out of a hat for you. Father has strict directions as to the sleight of hand necessary to guarantee you receive her choice for you."

Darcy threw his head back and pressed the bridge

of his nose with thumb and forefinger.

Such genuine thoughtfulness. He had done Lady Matlock a great disservice expecting so little from her. Assuming the best from people, even his own people, was clearly not his strong suit.

"I can see you are surprised."

Did Fitzwilliam have to look so pleased with himself?

"Aunt Matlock is indeed most gracious." He rubbed the back of his neck. "Whilst I appreciate the consideration, it does little to change the material fact that I am expected to perform!"

"She assures me that your character will require no performance on your part, merely act like yourself, and you will be 'in character' as it were. She has probably crafted Christopher Curmudgeon in your honor." Fitzwilliam swallowed back a laugh.

Best ignore that remark all together.

Darcy stalked across the room, following the faint track worn into the carpet. "I do appreciate her efforts, but still, I am denied my choice of partners for the evening. I must spend my time with whomever she draws from that ridiculous bag of hers."

"Everyone knows that it is a matter of chance. You are far too concerned—"

"No, I am not. You know full well how desperate the society gossips are to speculate on who I might or might not be involved with. Did you see the most recent entries?"

"No, actually, I missed the most recent round of that foolishness."

Darcy stomped to his desk and flung open a drawer. He snatched out a newspaper already folded open to the piece in question and thrust it at Fitzwilliam. "I burned the first copy, but thought I should retain the evidence to convince naysayers, such as yourself, of the very real dangers these harpies present."

Fitzwilliam grumbled and scanned the page. He muttered several colorful epithets that Darcy could just make out. Fitzwilliam always did have the most colorful oaths.

"Daft, feather-pated quill driver." He tossed the paper back into Darcy's hands. "Whatever did you do to make them so interested in you?"

"A single man of good fortune must be in want of a wife!" He snorted. "You may have my share of their attention if you wish."

"What, and encourage my mother to take a greater interest in my comings and goings? No, indeed. Still, you may take heart. Mother, in her great and magnanimous wisdom has also taken this concern under consideration."

Darcy returned the paper to his drawer and shut it with a bit more energy than he intended. "To what further machinations may I look forward?"

"She wishes me to assure you that if you but indicate a preference to her, she will contrive to make certain you have the partner you desire."

Darcy paced to the window and pressed his forehead against the cool glass. There in lay the problem. The partner he desired was not in London. Even if she were, her name would be completely unknown to any lofty personages. Dash it all! He could not even be seen with her in public without his life—and hers—coming under meticulous scrutiny. He pressed his temples.

Rot and nonsense! He must regulate his thoughts, not allow them to wander to her. She was most unsuitable in every way—fortune, breeding, connections, even her manners were barely adequate. And her family—truly appalling, nearly every one of them!

That was what he must focus on … not her fine eyes and informed, if pert, opinions. Not the exhilaration he found in conversation with her or the compelling way she challenged him to consider his own opinions.

He ran a finger along the inside of his cravat.

"Darcy?"

"There is no one I am interested in. I … I do not wish to be forced to spend the entire evening with any one young lady. People—including her family will get ideas, conveniently forgetting it was an act of chance alone that led me to being with her the first place." He threw his hands in the air.

"What about my sister? Letty is engaged, but her betrothed is on the continent right now. She has no need to use the opportunity to seek out an eligible man, so will miss nothing by being your companion. Not to mention, Lord Blake is known for his jealous streak and would not approve of Letty taking another partner for the evening. You, he will not perceive as a rival for Letty's attentions, thus keeping both of you safe."

"Jealous? But she has accepted his offer—"

Fitzwilliam shrugged. "I know. You need not convince me of the unseemliness of his attitude. Write to Blake yourself, you will see. The green-eyed monster is his own personal companion, following him everywhere like some demon spaniel. All I can say is that you would be doing Letty a favor as much as yourself."

Darcy stalked across the room and scratched the

back of his head. It was difficult to abandon the opportunity to be useful, particularly to one of his family. And Fitzwilliam was not exaggerating Lord Blake's jealousy.

"I suppose that would be acceptable." But, only barely.

Letty was not unintelligent, but her interests extended only so far as the *ton*. He would be forced to listen to her prattle on all evening about the latest *on-dit*. At least she would not be coy or flirtatious—and she would not expect him to call upon her the day after the ball.

Better still, her engagement ensured that the gossips would find their pairing of little interest. Exactly what he needed to make the night tolerable.

"So then, I may assure Mother you will come tonight?"

"I can tolerate an evening in your sister's company, but I will not—"

"Play any games, except a dignified rubber of whist." Fitzwilliam waved off his concerns. "Yes, yes, be assured, we all know that. I did not expect this would be the year we would see your face deep in a bullet pudding, or silently gesticulating a clue in charades."

Darcy shuddered. How did any find such pastimes amusing?

"You are fortunate. Letty prefers cards to other games as well. Be warned though, you may have to lower yourself and compromise to play commerce with her. She is notoriously bad at whist."

He had forgotten that. "I can accept the compromise."

"Very well then, I shall bring my mother the news

she most desires to hear." Fitzwilliam pushed to his feet in his slow effortless way that declared he had nary a care in the world. "I do not understand why she works so hard to see you come, nor why you say you will attend an event that you so clearly dread."

"Aunt Matlock requires my attendance because she wishes to see me married. She will take any opportunity to present me on the marriage mart, even if it is with your sister on my arm. I have no doubt she still hopes I might dance with some other young ladies and give her the credit of bringing me together with the partner of my future life." Darcy pressed his eyes with thumb and forefinger.

What would Aunt Matlock think, seeing him dance with the young lady he truly wished to partner? She would probably redouble her efforts and make Elizabeth the scorn of the *ton*. Aunt Matlock did not take well to upstarts and vulgar mushrooms, rising up in spheres to which they were not born.

Fitzwilliam sniggered. "Why do you put yourself through this when you could so easily decline?"

"It would be improper, impolite and ill-received to refuse her invitation."

Had he forgotten the force of nature Aunt Matlock became when someone attempted to gainsay her? Not to mention, it was required to honor Mother's memory.

"As you will." Fitzwilliam tipped his head and left.

Darcy returned to his desk and cradled his face in his hands. At least Fitzwilliam did not seem to suspect the underlying truth. He would be intolerable and persistent in his interrogations should he have any inkling as to the true object of Darcy's torment.

Still, politeness aside, Lady Matlock's invitation

might help him forget, even if for an evening. Letty's company, and constant chatter, had a way of distracting Darcy from any semblance of ordered thought.

At present, any distraction from the intruding memories of a charming Elizabeth Bennet was a welcome one, even if it was a Twelfth Night ball.

January 6, 1812 Twelfth Night. Meryton

Aunt Phillips hosted a Twelfth Night party, but had chosen to do so without consulting the Kings, who hosted a dinner and party of their own at the same time. It seemed little coincidence that all of the officers declined Aunt Phillips's invitation in favor of the Kings'. Though little different from last year's company, the gathering seemed drab and colorless. Lydia and Kitty felt the officers' loss keenly and loudly, especially after a few cups of punch. Finally, Papa intervened and suggested it was time that everyone returned home.

That had never happened before, and hopefully would never happen again.

Elizabeth trudged upstairs, if she could abscond to her room quickly enough, she might not be called upon to help Kitty and Lydia prepare for bed. Elizabeth's cheeks still burned for all they had said!

She wandered around her moonlit room. Sleep was not going to come soon. If only Jane were here to talk all this over with. But even if she had been, Jane would have been far too distressed for words right now.

Elizabeth lit several candles and pulled out her portable writing desk.

My dear Aunt Gardiner,

I hope this letter finds you well and warm this new year. Papa has had his first footer here to assure our future in the coming year. While I am not nearly so assured as he of our fortunes in the coming months, I do have news which I believe shall make for an agreeable start to the new year for you.

Concerning Mr. Wickham: I am now convinced, my dear aunt, that I have never been much in love; for had I really experienced that pure and elevating passion, I should at present detest his very name, and wish him all manner of evil. My watchfulness has been effectual; and though I should certainly be a more interesting object to all my acquaintance, were I distractedly in love with him, I cannot say that I regret my comparative insignificance.

Elizabeth paused and tapped her pen against her lips. Perhaps she had understated her feelings a bit to please her reader. More than just a bit really. But someone should get some pleasure out of the current turn of events. Moreover, Aunt Gardiner would probably be pleased to hear of his defection in favor of Mary King and her new fortune, but Mama's returning ill-humor and ill-health would be news far less well-received. With Charlotte's impending wedding there was little hope for improvement any time soon. Was it too soon to hope 1812 would conclude on a more agreeable note than it had begun?

January 7, 1812. London

The morning after Twelfth Night, Darcy blinked rheumy eyes, staring at the window, and trying to avoid the miserable brightness sneaking around the edges of the curtains. His head throbbed, stomach protesting like a mob rioting in the streets.

A mob would have been easier to quell.

He pressed his belly and smacked his lips. Drinking so much had been a poor choice, even if it had been in the privacy of his study, after the ball.

His study—he glanced about—he had slept in his study in his favorite leather wingback!

He squeezed his temples and groaned as fragments of memories came rushing into place.

On his return from the Matlock ball, he had intended to return to his chambers. The port in his study had called to him, though, one glass after another, until his best intentions faded away into an alcohol muddled haze. Port after several generous glasses of Aunt Matlock's famed—and very potent—punch was a very bad idea indeed.

The housekeeper pounded on the door.

Why did she feel the need to do that, today especially? A polite tap was all that had ever been needed to garner his attention. He would have to speak to her about that ... later.

The door squealed like a dying animal as she opened it. "Sir."

"What?" He clutched his temples and bit back the harsh words dancing on his tongue. There was no need for her to shout.

"I brought you something to help your ill-ease, some coffee, and a bite to eat if you wish it."

He flicked his hand toward a small table.

It would be a miracle if she did not crack every piece of porcelain on the tray with all the rattling and clattering. Was it possible to make more noise?

She shuffled out and slammed the door. The woman had never been so ungainly before—why now? He would have sharp words for her when—

His stomach roiled, and he reached for the glass, full of a slightly opaque liquid, sparkling in the too bright afternoon—afternoon?—light.

He shaded his eyes against the glare. How could it become afternoon so quickly?

He gulped down the contents of the glass.

Gah! With any good fortune, the drink would work better than it tasted. Not that it would be difficult. Could she not have provided him with something less foul than his temper?

He pitched forward and scrubbed his sandy eyes with his palms. If only he could scour away the previous night as well.

What a fool he had been, trusting Aunt Matlock would indeed make his evening tolerable. How clever of her to assign him and Letty the bard's Benedick and Beatrice, so, in her words 'their debates and disagreeable remarks would be entirely in character.' How kind and generous her assessment of him.

Perhaps she meant it as a joke.

He gulped down another mouthful of the housekeeper's foul tonic.

At least the costumes had been tolerable, an officer's coat for him and a wreath of flowers for her. Acceptable enough.

The evening began to unravel after his second cup of punch, happily provided by Letty herself. Had she been trying to relax him, or provoke him? It was difficult to tell, and either would have been in keeping with her character.

She had been pleased enough with her role for the

evening. Of course, she would relish the opportunity to disagree with him at every turn. What was more natural than her doing nearly all the talking for them both?

Then she chanced upon the great fun in pointing out every woman in the room, attractive or not and remarking upon her assets and flaws. The punch made him careless. When he flinched upon her mention of fine eyes, she made that the target of her future remarks. Over and over, he was forced to observe fine eyes.

That only served to remind him that the pair of fine eyes he truly desired to see were situated hours away, and unwelcome at such an affair in any event.

As his temper grew worse, Letty delighted in her success. She knew the bard's work too well and perceived precisely how to draw him in.

At one point, in a futile attempt at distraction, he had politely remarked upon the weather—the weather!—only to receive her response:

"I wonder that you will still be talking, Signior Benedick: nobody marks you."

"What, my dear Lady Disdain! Are you yet living?"

The words slipped out before he could control them, and the game, for Letty was on.

"Is it possible disdain should die while she hath such meet food to feed it as Signior Benedick? Courtesy itself must convert to disdain, if you come in her presence."

Heat rose along his jaw—or perhaps it was the punch. How dare she insult his deportment! It was not to be borne.

"Then is courtesy a turncoat. But it is certain I am loved of all ladies, only you excepted: and I would I could find in my heart that I had not a hard heart; for, truly, I love none."

Why had he permitted himself those words? Even playing a role, he disdained to lie. What was Elizabeth driving him to?

Letty, though, took far too much delight in his protest.

The look she had given him as she said, *"A dear happiness to women: they would else have been troubled with a pernicious suitor. I thank God and my cold blood. I am of your humor for that: I had rather hear my dog bark at a crow than a man swear he loves me."*

Her betrothed would be pleased with that public declaration. Perhaps it was made for the benefit of the nearby tell-alls who would repeat the evening's most flavorful morsels to anyone who heard them. But something in her eyes implied she enjoyed the lines too much for it to be merely an act.

"God keep your ladyship still in that mind! So some gentleman or other shall 'scape a predestinate scratched face."

"Scratching could not make it worse, an 'twere such a face as yours were."

That was uncalled for, even if the bard had written it. Elizabeth would have twisted the line somehow, with something witty and clever, and entirely her own. Even in the moments her wit was most sharp, she did not stoop to vulgar insults and would not even for the sake of the script.

He gulped the remainder of his punch.

In retrospect, perhaps not the wisest choice. That glass burned all the way down, spreading a fiery boldness through his belly.

"Well, you are a rare parrot-teacher."

"A bird of my tongue is better than a beast of yours." Letty laughed, a shrill, ear-splitting sound on the best of days which had clearly not improved with drink.

"I would my horse had the speed of your tongue, and so good a continuer. But keep your way, i' God's name; I have done."

Oh, she had not liked that, given the face she made at him. *"You always end with a jade's trick: I know you of old."*

Had she but a modicum of restraint, it might have been bearable. She shrieked and carried on as though those words were meant personally, not written for the public's entertainment. It was easy enough for her to dole out the bard's words, but to be on the receiving end of them—that was intolerable.

He scrubbed his face with his hands. Great heavens, even the Bennet family had checked themselves better! Was it possible that family demonstrated greater decorum than his own?

That was not possible. What would Lydia Bennet have done with the character of Beatrice? He shuddered.

Heavens! That thought must have been the result of far too much port.

He leaned back in his chair and threw his arm over his eyes. His own behavior left much to be desired. Had he only followed his own advice, Letty's tantrum might have been avoided. One might easily argue, it had been entirely his fault.

Fitzwilliam would not see it that way, but surely an unpleasant call from Aunt Matlock was in the offing. He could hardly blame her. Mother would not have approved of his behavior. Elizabeth would probably not have been impressed either.

Even with Letty's outrageous conduct, his plan for the ball had largely been a success, at least until this moment. He had hardly thought about Elizabeth Bennet during the entire evening. Not when the young Miss Blake, wearing the gown that would have better suited Miss Elizabeth, sauntered past. Not when the musicians played the same music he and Elizabeth had danced to at Netherfield. Not when he caught a glimpse of the library on the way to the card room, and the same book Miss Elizabeth read while she stayed at Netherfield captured his gaze. Not when Letty attempted to involve him in conversation with her shallow chatter and gossip that bored him senseless instead of endeavoring to engage him in sensible discourse. None of those moments made him consider Miss Elizabeth at all.

It was only now in the solitude of his study that thoughts of that maddening woman invaded his consciousness, refusing to give way in the face of his stalwart defenses.

Why was it no young lady, regardless of fortune, connections, or beauty, seemed to measure up to the standard set by the impertinent Hertfordshire miss?

There had to be something for this untoward distraction—something other than a stay in Bedlam. He leaned back and closed his eyes.

"What is troubling you, dear?" Mother gathered her skirts and sat beside him on the uppermost step of the grand stair.

Darcy shrugged. "Nothing."

She leaned her shoulder against his. "Nothing often bothers me as well."

She had always been so understanding. What would she have said about Elizabeth?

Elizabeth was a woman who had nothing, absolutely nothing to recommend her, but herself. Nothing but her wit, her kindness, her devotion to her family, her reputation in the community, her beauty, her manners … all those things Mother had considered cardinal virtues.

Was Elizabeth worth the scorn it might cost him?

Aunt Matlock would insist she was not. Likely the rest of the family would agree.

But Mother, she would say she was.

A cool swath of peace settled over his shoulders and wrapped around him, bandaging all the worn and ragged places of his soul.

Of course, of course! It was so clear, so simple.

He would not forget her. Somehow, someday, he would see her again, and when he did, he would make her an offer of marriage. Then all would finally be right with the world..

Epilogue

JANE AUSTEN WROTE that on this same day Jane visits Miss Bingley at Grosvenor Street—a visit not well appreciated by the recipient to be sure. Two days later, on January 9, Charlotte married Mr. Collins and Jane Austen picks up the narrative once again.

Do these scenes represent what Austen conceived of for her characters during Christmastide 1811? One will really never know, perhaps they do not, but then again, it is pleasing to think that they might.

Acknowledgments

So many people have helped me along the journey taking this from an idea to a reality.

Anji, Julie, and Debbie thank you so much for cold reading, proof reading and being honest!

And my dear friend Cathy, my biggest cheerleader, you have kept me from chickening out more than once!

And my sweet sister Gerri who believed in even those first attempts that now live in the file drawer!

Thank you!

Other Books by Maria Grace

Remember the Past
The Darcy Brothers

Given Good Principles Series:

Darcy's Decision
The Future Mrs. Darcy
All the Appearance of Goodness
Twelfth Night at Longbourn

Jane Austen's Dragons Series:

Pemberley: Mr. Darcy's Dragon
Longbourn: Dragon Entail

The Queen of Rosings Park Series:

Mistaking Her Character
The Trouble to Check Her
A Less Agreeable Man

Sweet Tea Stories:

A Spot of Sweet Tea: Hopes and Beginnings (short story anthology)
A Spot of Sweet Tea: Hopes and Beginnings: Christmastide tales (Christmas novella anthology)

Darcy & Elizabeth: Chrismas 1811
The Darcy's First Christmas

From Admiration to Love
Snowbound at Hartfield

Regency Life (Nonfiction) Series:

A Jane Austen Christmas: Regency Christmas Traditions
Courtship and Marriage in Jane Austen's World

Short Stories:

Four Days in April
Sweet Ginger
Last Dance
Not Romantic

Available in paperback, e-book, and audiobook format at all online bookstores.

On Line Exclusives at:

www.http//RandomBitsofFascination.com

Bonus and deleted scenes
Regency Life Series

<u>Free e-books</u>:
Bits of Bobbin Lace
The Scenes Jane Austen Never Wrote: First Anniversaries
Half Agony, Half Hope: New Reflections on Persuasion
Four Days in April
Jane Bennet in January
February Aniversaries

About the Author

Though Maria Grace has been writing fiction since she was ten years old, those early efforts happily reside in a file drawer and are unlikely to see the light of day again, for which many are grateful. After penning five file-drawer novels in high school, she took a break from writing to pursue college and earn her doctorate in Educational Psychology. After 16 years of university teaching, she returned to her first love, fiction writing.

She has one husband and one grandson, two graduate degrees and two black belts, three sons, four undergraduate majors, five nieces, is starting her sixth year blogging on Random Bits of Fascination, has built seven websites, attended eight English country dance balls, sewn nine Regency era costumes, and shared her life with ten cats.

She can be contacted at:

author.MariaGrace@gmail.com

Facebook:
http://facebook.com/AuthorMariaGrace

On Amazon.com:
http://amazon.com/author/mariagrace

Random Bits of Fascination
(http://RandomBitsofFascination.com)

Austen Variations (http://AustenVariations.com)

English Historical Fiction Authors
 (http://EnglshHistoryAuthors.blogspot.com)

White Soup Press (http://whitesouppress.com/)

On Twitter @WriteMariaGrace

On Pinterest: http://pinterest.com/mariagrace423/